I'll Never Forget

An Anthology by the

Monash Writers Group

Tale

First Published 2025

All writing is fictional and doesn't refer to any living or dead person, except where noted.

National Library of Australia Cataloguing-in-Publication entry
Creator: Monash Writers Group, author.
Title: I'll Never Forget: Monash Writers Anthology.
ISBN: 9781763836808 (paperback)
Subjects: short stories.
Cover design by Robert New

Tale Publishing
Melbourne Victoria

Also by the

Monash Writers Group

The Way Forward

Unprecedented Times

The Last Line

The First Line

View from the Hill

Introduction

Fiction

A Wagon-Load of Wool by **Lenette Griffin**   1
The Love Procedure by **Robert New**   25
Angle of Repose by **R Andrew Russell**   47
Fireflies by **Erica Tippett**   61

Poetry

Love & I'll Never Forget by **Robert Eisler**   89
I Will Never Forget Poems by **Katharina Fares**
97
Waiting by the Phone, Ode to Struggling Writers
& A Young Storyteller by **Sung-Ju Suya Lee** 113
Japan & The Bride by **Dilys Smith**   119

Memoir

I'll Never Forget by **Sakuntala Gananathan** 125
I'll Never Forget: Summers in Melbourne by
Marlene Laurent   129
The Coronation Of Queen Elizabeth ll by
Gordon Smith   151
I'll Never Forget… My Grandad is Sleeping…
by **Premila Thurairatnam**   165

About the Authors

Introduction

Welcome to the latest Monash Writers Group's anthology. It is hard to believe that we've now published a half dozen anthologies. Choosing a theme was quite a difficult task this time round, as we wanted a more timeless theme in comparison to our last two anthologies which centred around the pandemic which drastically altered our lives between 2020 and 2022. Even though our theme, I'll Never Forget, could easily slot into the pandemic theme, our authors have written stories, poetry and memoir which are not anchored to that time.

We have a diverse membership, and our authors have written in a variety of genres. We hope you appreciate the diversity of the works here.

Any book like this requires input from many people; thanks go to our editor, Sarah Lemcke from All in the Edit, for elevating our work with feedback on drafts and proofreading the final manuscript.

None of this would have been possible

without the support of the Monash City Libraries and Monash City Council, who sponsor and promote the Writers Group.

Thank you to the members of the Monash Writers Group. Your support of the anthology and desire to see it come to fruition has been inspirational.

Lastly, thank you dear reader. We hope you enjoy reading this collection as much as we have in putting it together.

Robert New
Chair, Monash Writers Group

Fiction

A Wagon-Load of Wool.
Lenette Griffin

Lately, the memory curls around me like a wisp of autumn smoke from the forest burn-off. Sometimes, a shred of ephemeral silvery blue twisting vapour moved by an invisible breeze, sometimes rich with the scent of burnt lavender and golden burnished colour, sometimes, a puff of breath, teasing at the edges of an almost-thought.

But always, no matter how infrequently the pungent pulse emerges, it brings with it a sharp pang of—regret? Loss? No. A dark, insistent pressure to tell the tale which weighed like a millstone, dormant in the old man's head, for seventy, almost eighty years.

My visit to the nursing home today would be like every other one of late, I expected. Make a brief scan of his tiny room with its mechanical hospital-style bed, the practical chair with sturdy arms for lifting himself up and the pale green upholstery with its old, faded stains. The dark-brown laminated corner unit with a hodgepodge collection of tiny photos in frames, a gilded box which held all his treasures, some worn books occasionally neatly stacked, today not so much. Not a lot of evidence to mark a rich and vibrant lifestyle.

I check the clothes drawers but there is nothing to see. The staff have folded his meagre collection with the usual military precision, like the bright cover on his bed. Knife-edge tucks, perfectly plumped pillow, antiseptic scoured bathroom, all pristine and gleaming in the white light. Sterile and impersonal. Although he's lived in this room for six years or more.

I chatter away while I move aimlessly around, holding the belief that the sound of my voice will be welcome, if not meaningful for him, although he doesn't usually know who I am gossiping about. I tell him about my children and their families, all of whom live either interstate or, in Cameron's case, overseas. Most of the stories are true but when I run out of content, I make them up. Not that that happens often. Or I embellish the ones I've already told him. I ignore the fact that he could go into the lounge and stare at different walls, but he doesn't want that. Too noisy, he claims, but I think he can't bear to see all those other oldies reflecting his own forlorn fate back at him.

He doesn't remember any of his own children, or their children. There are a few school photos cluttered on the shelf but none of the miserable devils ever visit, to remind him, so why would he remember? Bet they come out of the woodwork when he passes on though.

He doesn't speak much anymore. Perhaps he doesn't have anything left to say, or can't remember how to speak. Perhaps he tells his stories in his own mind where he dwells, staring into space for most of the day. He does mutter away to himself sometimes. The disease is like that.

"I'll bring in another album on Tuesday," I chirp brightly at him, "and we can look through all those old pictures from the farm—remember the big floods when you lost all those sheep after the silly sods didn't have the sense to move further up the hill?"

He nods slowly. "Yes," he says.

"Would you like me to take you out onto the deck and we can sit in the sun for a while and have some hot Milo to warm us up?" It's actually quite warm but the poor old fellow feels the cold terribly. His circulation system is shot to blazes.

"Not yet," he answers, his voice suddenly clear and firm, and he shuffles in his seat to sit up a little higher. "I have to tell you something and I don't want *them* to know," he jerks his head towards the door—'them' meaning the staff, I suppose.

"Oh sure. What is it, Tom? What's bothering you?" I perch on the end of the bed, waiting, never quite sure what will come out of his mouth. Often, it's something trivial, like he can't find his glasses or handkerchiefs because 'the people steal everything around here'. Sometimes, when he has moments of near-lucidity he's desperate to escape 'this blasted prison.' And sometimes, all too often, 'it' is a figment of his imagination—"Mind all that water, the place has been flooded so I'll just go and get a mop"—the sunlight slanting across the floors usually triggers that.

"It's always worried me," he says now, frowning with fierce concentration, "and I have to tell someone before I forget. Before I die. It has to be told." He's speaking clearly and deliberately, no sign of a mumble and his eyes are bright and looking straight into mine, totally aware.

Well, this is new. He hasn't been this alert for a year, maybe more.

"What has to be told?"

"They killed the Chinaman. The two of them."

"*What?* Who killed somebody?" He seems so serious, and I'm startled out of my wits now.

"When we took a load of wool to the saleyards one time. Our wool was always the best fine Merino but we didn't have a full wagon-load that year and neither did anyone else in the district but we always shared and the two Harry's rounded up enough of their own to go with it. Harry Murphy's wagon was a bit bigger than my father's, so he was the driver, although his horses weren't up to much. He was a mean bugger and never looked after his machinery or his stock. Well, they were bits of scruffy bush brumbies he caught and broke in. He never owned a well-bred horse in his life, far as I know. Anyway, we had a team of four horses when we should have had six. It wasn't the horses' fault that they were half starved and not strong enough for the job. I really can't remember why dad didn't send his own horses. He sent me along though—often contracted me out because my labour was cheaper than a grown man." Tom creased his brow in thought.

I sit, wondering where this story was going and whether I'll get to the bank before it closes. He never talks too long before he falls asleep.

"But yes, I do know why. Neither of those Harrys looked after their stock—they were cruel blokes, and dad wouldn't want them to abuse any of his fine Drysdales. We had some of the best work horses in the district, you know. Some of the best riding hacks too." He trailed off for a moment and I thought that was it.

Yes, I do know. I knew from the stories

my dad used to tell that Tom was a wonderful, fearless rider as a young man and I even remembered seeing him on his farm once when I was little, riding at full gallop across a paddock as if he and the horse were one. I thought he was a hero.

"It was a good trip, even though it was so slow because the horses needed resting quite often. I was happy to sit on a chaff-bag and my swag high up behind the Harrys and just look at the bush as we passed through. The smell of the wool and the sweat of the horses is like nothing you've ever smelt. Never got it out of my system. And the bush smells—ah, those big gums—God, they're the kings of the earth. The tobacco from their pipes had a strong smell too, nothing clean, like the bush, but I didn't mind it, although I never took up smoking myself. The two Harrys both smoked pipes like chimneys but they wouldn't have offered me a puff even if I'd wanted one. They were mean as snakes and I was only a kid. I think I was about fourteen or fifteen and I'd been working since I was, gee, about twelve, I guess. Wasn't tall but I was wiry back then, and strong. Life on the farm was tough and some of the work I did on other farms was even harder. Conditions were harsh for everyone in those days.

"It took us a full four days back then, to get down to the market. They took me along as their rouseabout, so I looked after the horses and made sure we had enough wood for the fire when we made camp at night. I couldn't manage a wool-bale on my own of course, but I could scramble up on the top of the load to undo the ropes and help one of the men to push them down. You had to be pretty sure of your balance up there—the bales were stacked three or four rows high, and the wagon floor was already higher than my shoulder. I could use the grappling hooks, although my hands weren't full size, so they ached after a day of hauling bales. Those hooks were vicious things, metal, with two loops for your thumb and fingers to fit through and the three big spikes as the claws. My hands were hardened up but they barely stretched across then. They were made to fit a man's hand.

"At night, after I'd fed and watered the

horses and got the fire going and got some water for the billycan and a pot for whatever meat we threw in, then it was easy going. They always set a couple of rabbit traps and then we'd sit around the fire and the two Harrys would smoke their pipes while they tried to outdo each other with their yarns, most of which would've been lies I reckon. Harry Murphy was my father's cousin—second or third, I think, and he was a bit of a rough type. Crude language and no manners around the ladies. Never went to school but he could write his name and still reckoned he knew everything. Lived on his wits when he wasn't scratching a living on the few acres he owned a few miles from our farm. Life would have been miserable for his wife, I think. Don't remember her.

"Harry Brown, now he was a really bad fella and he was known far and wide as a thief although there was never any evidence whenever the constables rode into town so he never went to jail. Somehow, he used to get a tip-off or something and shoot through just before they'd ride in. He'd pinch anything that wasn't nailed down. He was married and had a half-dozen kids but they and his wife didn't see much of him. I don't think that was his real name either. My dad reckoned different people knew his as some other names and I wouldn't be surprised. He was a real ladies' man," Tom grinned *(first time he's done that in ages!)* and chuckled, "although, for the life of me, I can't think what they saw in him.

"Anyway, I never liked him even before then. And after that trip I hated him. Both of 'em." He sighed and shifted his gaze to me. "It's a heavy weight, you know, to hate someone that much, and for almost your whole life. When the hate's born out of fear though, it's hard to get rid of. And part of that hate is because I always felt guilty, not for what I did but for what they did. And y' can't be responsible for what other men do, 'specially evil men, I know that, but somehow you still do."

"What happened on that trip?" I ask now. Because I'm fully intrigued by this insight into Tom as a young man and also still trying to determine if he's dreamed up some fantasy.

And, damn it, I want to know if it *is* real.

"Oh, we took the load down to the saleyards at the port. For a young kid who'd never been anywhere much, that was a real excitement, seeing the sea for the first time in my life and so many people. Men swearing, horses and wagons and carts everywhere. I couldn't work out how they all knew where they were going and how they didn't all crash into each other. There were big mobs of cattle being brought in too because the cattle yards were nearby and it was thrilling to see all those fine beasts. I think that's where I first got my interest in cattle breeding. They seemed such majestic, sensible creatures, compared to the sheep my dad always carried.

"Anyhow, we didn't hang around the port too long after we unloaded the bales, although Harry Brown kicked up a stink because he knew where the brothels were and wanted to go there—not that I knew what they were at that stage—but they argued awhile and settled for spending a few hours in a seedy pub while I amused myself watching all the activity and listening to the men talk. There were hardly any women about so the language was pretty rough. I asked one man about his cattle and he spoke to me for a while, and told me about their breed, they were Hereford shorthorns. He gave me an apple and it was the best thing I'd tasted since we left the farm. We might have been at that port for days if Harry Murphy didn't dig his heels in. They came busting out of the pub well before the six o'clock closing and yelled at me to get the horses hitched in a hurry so we could start out before dark. From the bits of conversation I heard once we got moving, I guessed that the other Harry, Harry Brown, got into some type of trouble inside and had to clear out quick— tried to rob a bloke somehow or pick his pocket. I didn't get told but we had a rough camp that night because it was too late to get far into the hills and the moon hadn't risen.

"I've always liked to sleep under the stars if I can. Just stretch out in the swag near the fire and listen to the night sounds in the bush. You know, there's always possums grunting about in the trees, and insects scuffling about or the 'roos thumping about—they never come near the fire—but the dingoes are not afraid of anything. They'll come right up close, into the light and just stand there, very still, watching. And the sky is always just that much closer when you're looking up at it from the swag… all those twinkling stars… the moon big and bright and yellow.

"After that next night though, to hell with the stars. I crawled right in under the wagon and slept there, not that that would have stopped them from killing me, if they decided to. Still didn't sleep much for the rest of the trip. Thankfully, with the wagon empty it was a quicker trip, although the horses were tired. We caught two rabbits in the traps too, so had some fresh meat which we roasted over the coals and tea for the billy so that was a pretty good dinner.

"As camps go, it wasn't the best, but the two Harrys knew it from previous trips and there was a bit of a gully with fresh water unless it was late summer and always plenty of rabbits not to go hungry. Plus, the occasional 'roo would come down for a drink. I don't think they had guns with us but we could've wrapped a boomerang around one if we needed a bigger lot of meat. They talked about it but then didn't bother and I wished we had got one because we all had dogs to feed. And mum liked kangaroo tail soup—everybody did. It was a nice change from rabbit." He pursed his lips, drifting off, and I feel a brief burst of panic—*don't stop now!*

"What about the Chinaman?" I ask loudly, hoping to jog his memory before he goes to sleep.

"Mmm? Oh… yeah. They killed the poor fellow. Murdered him."

"Why?"

The hair on the back of my neck is frizzing like a shorting fuse and I'm shivering. *I think this actually happened.*

"Greed, I s'pose. Just—bloody, cold-hearted greed."

"How?" *Come on, don't lose it now Tom, I have to know.*

"Well… it was a fairly warm day I remember, so we spelled the horses a couple of times more than usual. Harry Murphy got a sudden concern to care for his animals I guess, or maybe he worked out if they died we'd all have to walk home. Would've done 'em both good," he muttered.

In the silence, Maureen, one of the nurses, opened the door and looked in. "All good Tom?" I nod at her because Tom stays mute. "You look comfy so I'll bring your drink in here, Tom. Like a cuppa?" she turns to me and I could just about kiss her. "Thank you. I'd kill for a coffee, no sugar." *Ah, hell—bad choice of words.*

But killing's suddenly on my mind. Another shiver ripples down my spine.

I'm so grateful when a young, dark-eyed girl whom I haven't seen before enters without knocking and brings our drinks—Tom's is flavoured milk, I notice—and a plate of fresh biscuits. Fantastic! If I run into the toilet, will he lose his train of thought and fall asleep? He may never remember it again. I consider the thought for thirty seconds, then reject it.

"Wish I had."

"What's that, Tom? What did you wish you had?"

"Walked home that day. When I woke up

and realised what they'd done."

"How did you realise they did that, Tom?" Despite the coffee I'm shivering visibly now and my blood has curdled. 'Cause I'm pretty sure he's telling me a true story.

"We got into the clearing where we were camping just before sundown and I ran around unharnessing the horses, getting their hobbles and putting their nosebags on, while the Harrys walked about and collected a few sticks to start the fire. Harry Brown went off to set the rabbit traps and check things out.

"There was a big swamp not far from the camp and, close to where the drays and wagons always pulled up, a reedy waterhole where we could water the horses. There was a bit of slime in close to the bank but once you skimmed that back from the surface, the water underneath was clear and sweet. I think it was fed from a spring near the middle of the waterhole. There was a mighty-long limestone ridge not far to the east so the run-off would come from there.

"Anyway, I went off to fill the billycan and have a quick wash before it got too late and cold. The damn water in that swamp was always freezing. When I looked up, I saw a cart a couple of hundred yards away pulled up under some trees, and a skinny horse hobbled just near it. The cart was piled high with a load of dried possum skins, and a few rabbit skins. There was a pokey little fire already alight. We hadn't realised anyone else was there, 'cause usually blokes would come out when you stopped anywhere, and the jingling of the harnesses and the men's voices would carry through the bush long before we came into view. I thought the bloke must be scouting about for wood, or just checking the layout of the land so found a solid stick and I dug around in the soft mud along the banks where I saw a lot of nice healthy wild irises. They had fat juicy bulbs which we used to cook like potatoes, and these looked super sweet. I learned very young how to live on bush tucker.

"I washed them and myself again and as I stood up I saw the man watching me. He was tiny and very brown, with the traditional long pigtail braided down his back and he had a straw—what do you call it—coolie hat dangling from a string around his neck so I knew straight away he was a Chinaman. He nodded but didn't speak and he didn't come any closer, so I gave him a nod and a wave back and took my water and the bulbs back to our fire. I still had to round up enough wood for the night so I kept busy until dark and thought it best not to mention our neighbour to the Harrys. He would have come over if he wanted company, I assumed.

"It wasn't unusual to see other men at the waterholes. Often there were swaggies or men looking for work or just walking to the city if they didn't have a horse. People, 'specially in the country, were all poor in those days right after the Great Depression. The Chinaman probably spent months at a time in the bush, trapping animals and drying their skins. There was a fair price on good quality skins, but it was still a damned hard way to scratch a living.

"The rabbit stew tasted all the better for adding the lily bulbs and I was happy to sit on a log after we'd eaten while the two Harrys puffed their pipes and told their yarns and scuffed the dirt with their hob-nail boots. 'Saw a Chinaman down the other side,' Harry Murphy said after a while. 'Has a cart load of skins that look pretty good.' 'Zat right?' the other Harry said. 'Where would he get those, I wonder. Maybe he stole 'em. Good money in skins now.' 'There'd be a fair few quid in that load he's got—I wonder if he'd sell it?' Harry Murphy said. Nothing more was said about it, but they gave each other a few looks which I didn't like. They didn't seem in much of a hurry to move out in the morning and after a while Harry Brown took himself off towards the waterhole. Harry Murphy wandered away too, and I didn't think much of it at first but the two of them came back shortly, leading the little horse and its cart piled high with skins. There was no sign of the Chinaman, and I got very uneasy. When I asked what was going on, they both found other things to look at and Harry Brown gave one of his nasty grins. 'I found this poor little pony left to die, with no food, and the whole of this load was just left abandoned. Thought I should rescue the little fella.'

'Where's the Chinaman?' I asked and

Harry Murphy spoke up. 'Dunno. We looked around for him but he seems to have done a runner. Must'a left and abandoned all this. Perhaps he's running from the law and got frightened or some'ing.' He snorted at his own joke. I must have looked as sceptical as I felt because they were lying and not even trying to do a very good job of it. 'Yeah, I reckon he must've gone for a pee in the night and got lost and fallen into one of the old mine shafts,' Harry Brown sniggered, 'Might'a broke his neck.'"

Tom sighed heavily and took a sip of his milk, seeming to notice it for the first time. I had left him one biscuit but he doesn't want it so I break it in half and hand a piece to him. He shakes his head, sadly. I eat the other half.

"I asked what they did to him, but they both said 'Nothing' in a way which would have convinced me they did something, even if I wasn't already suspicious. I stood my ground for a bit, wondering what I could do but it was pretty clear I couldn't do anything and I was feeling really sick as they walked around and around that little cart, sneering at each other.

"After a couple of minutes, Harry Murphy started hitching the little horse to the back of the wagon and I was shaking like a leaf as the shock set in. 'I'm going to go and look for him,' I told them, 'and you can go if you want.'

"'Better think about that again kid,' Harry Brown said. 'Far as we can tell there's no sign of that China-fella and we've found this load, all by ourselves in the bush, so I say he's run off and it's finders keepers. You don't want to cause us to get in trouble with your dad, if we don't bring you back safe and sound now, do you? And hanging around here looking for a dead fella's not getting us anywhere. Now, you get your little arse up on that wagon and let's get moving.' 'Yeah, you get up now, Tom,' Harry Murphy added, a bit softer, 'No point in worryin' about things that can't be changed. He's long gone, I reckon.' And he gave me a good shove towards the wagon. 'Horses are getting shifty and so am I.' The two Harrys climbed up, and Harry Murphy flipped the reins and we lumbered off back to the track.

"I didn't have anything to say, I was just numbed to the bone but eventually, after they'd shared some other scary looks at each other, Harry Murphy spoke to me over his shoulder. 'When we sell this lot Tom, there should be a few bob in it for you, you know. Best not to say anything to anyone though about where it came from, y'understand?'

"I told him to keep the filthy money but I was frightened so bad, I hardly moved the rest of the way. I couldn't get off that wagon fast enough and I told my father when I got home that I would never go anywhere with either of them again. Then when he held out four shillings to pay me for my work, I refused to take it. It was the first time I ever defied my father and I never told him why. I suppose he worked out some of it though, because the cartload of skins would have been a dead giveaway, and he knew those mongrels' reputations from way back.

"He never asked me about it so I figured he didn't want to know and when I considered all the options, I didn't think it would do any good to make a ruckus. There were no police in the region and I knew if anything ever came out I'd be the next one to end up down a mineshaft or a well. And who would listen to a boy when those black-hearted killers would have sworn blind that nothing happened? Or worse, that I was involved?

"It was a long time before I could sleep at night though. He was just a man. Working hard, minding his own business, and those two did that. How could anyone, any decent human being, do that…"

He trails off, rubbing his gnarly hands as if to warm them. "Had to tell the poor fellow's story. He deserved for it to be told. Had to tell someone before I die." His rheumy old eyes meet mine apologetically, while I sit, frozen and stunned. I fidget with my wedding ring, twisting and twisting it around my finger, turning all that over in my head. When I look back at him, his head is bent forward and he's asleep.

When I go to see him the next week with the album and a picture book of horses, as promised, I was told at the nurse's station that Tom had passed peacefully away in his sleep on Saturday. No one could let me know because I was not family and with the privacy rules, blah, blah, blah.

~

It's six years now since Tom told me his story.

Long enough ago that the memory has dissolved from the murky brown mass of horror which I learned about so abruptly and which kept me sleepless for many nights and unsettled for weeks. Time has again curled the fragments of dark knowledge into almost invisible, blue-white tendrils of smoke, drifting and mischievous, a quicksilver thread of brutality which darts into dreams in the middle of a restless night or lurks about in the subconscious, to sour the memories of a gentle man who passed his dangerous secret on to me.

He deserved for it to be told…

Perhaps those wisps will coalesce now with other memory fragments of regret and sorrow, and will turn warm and forgiven and golden and be carried away on a benevolent breeze. And be gone forever, like a nameless Chinaman. And Tom.

He deserved for it to be told…

The Love Procedure
Robert New

"Dad died last week." The words caught in Aaron's throat. It was painful to say aloud. Aaron trembled as he gripped the lectern. The auditorium was packed with people mourning their friend. Aaron was sure his loss was greater. How could he explain how in awe of his father he'd been?

"The autopsy revealed an undiagnosed, benign tumour pressing on his medulla. He died in his sleep. He'd been dizzy a lot recently, but put it down to doing too much, and not getting enough rest. But that's how Dad was, always doing several things at once."

Aaron paused and noted several nods from the audience.

"But you all knew him, and the other speakers have already covered who he was as a friend and colleague, so I thought I would/should talk about him as a parent…"

Aaron willed the words to come out of his suddenly concrete throat.

"My dad would say he wasn't a great dad, just a good one and that he was okay with that. I'd disagree. When it came to the small stuff, sure, he could be as impatient as anyone, but for the bigger stuff, he was awesome, even great and that's what I can't stop thinking about now."

Aaron glanced at Anushka, his recent love, and wondered how she'd feel about him being about to talk about an ex-girlfriend. After a few recent arguments, Aaron was beginning to wonder if Anushka was beginning to aspire to that status.

"To illustrate; I'll never forget that when I was fifteen, I was invited to go to a movie with some friends. Dad dropped me off. When he picked me up, he waited until we were on a main road, so we didn't have to look at each other, then hit me with, 'You know Sophie likes you.'"

~

"What?" Aaron shifted in his seat. "Why would you say that?"

"Ooh, you like her too, otherwise you would have said no she doesn't."

"*Daaad*," Aaron groaned.

"I could tell, 'cos when I dropped you off, she was standing further away from Virat and Tommy than they were to each other. Plus, when you approached, she took a half step towards you—probably unconsciously."

"So?"

"She was there because of you. You said Virat organised this. I bet if you ask him, she only said yes once she realised you'd be part of the group. I tell you what, organise another movie for next weekend, but offer for me to give her a lift home. I'll bet she'll jump at it. Then, if that works, when we drop her off, walk her to her door and say maybe next time we go out it could be just the two of us. Listen carefully to the tone of her reply. If it's excited, you're in, even more so if she asks "like a date?" If she says that, say yes. Be confident."

"There's a problem."

The car pulled up abruptly at some traffic lights. Aaron realised his dad was concentrating more on him than the road but trying not to show it.

"Virat likes her."

"Do you like her?" His dad countered.

Aaron said he did. His dad paused. He always did when he was about to say something he thought was important—his way of making sure you were paying attention. In this case he made a point of looking Aaron in the eye.

"She gets to choose. Even if she's so prized, she's not a prize to be won. Right?"

"Yeah, I get it, Dad."

"Talk to Virat. Say you like her too. Say you want to ask her out. If he thinks she likes him not you, he'll think she'll say no, and give you the okay. Sell it to him that if she says no, she'll most likely say it's because she likes someone else. You'll ask if it's Virat, if she says yes, you'll be his wingman… and *mean* it."

"Won't he think I'm stabbing him in the back? I mean he knows I know he likes her."

"True friends stab you in the front."

"Huh?"

"If you want to maintain a friendship with Virat, don't do anything behind his back. He may be pissed if you get the girl, but that's a repairable situation. If you go behind his back, it's a betrayal. That sort of thing can end friendships. Believe me, I know."

"Why can't girls just tell you how they feel?"

Aaron's dad grinned and replied wistfully, "Shy girls will spend a lot of time near you. Confident girls won't tell you they like you; they'll just find a way to talk to you every day."

~

Aaron looked at his audience. "That was when the scales fell from my eyes. Sophie always said hello to me and always asked me about something. *Each, and every day.*" Aaron was careful not to add it was how he'd recognised Anushka liked him too. "Dad just knew stuff like that and could read a situation better than most. Dad then offered to pay for both of us to see the movie, including snacks, on the condition he got to pick which movie we saw. I agreed, mostly because I was too dumbfounded to argue. I asked Dad if he could always spot such things. He said he had to be looking for them. It was a skill that spent much of the time turned off. 'But,' he added, 'I'll always know if you lie to me. I might not always call you on it, though. You're a teenager, you're entitled to some secrets, but I'll know.'"

~

Aaron's voice was hoarse, and he fought back tears. "I think that was the moment I realised I loved my dad. I'd said it to him lots before. But in that moment, I admired him so much. He became my hero, especially since he was spot on with his assessment and how things played out. I dated Sophie for six months—an eternity for a teenage relationship. I'm pleased to say that fifteen years later, Virat, Sophie, Tommy and I are all still friends. They're even here today."

Aaron gestured to the back of the room, where his friends were sitting. The packed hall dutifully looked around. Sophie gave a half wave.

Aaron was grateful the crowd had turned away, as the enormity of his loss overwhelmed him, and he couldn't hold back the tears any longer. Without finishing his speech, he walked slowly off the stage, while whispering, "I love you, Dad."

~

Three days later Aaron went with his mother and younger brother, Graham, to his dad's lawyer's office for the reading of the will. Aaron was due to meet Anushka that evening, but he wasn't sure if she'd suggested a dinner date because she was just being a supportive girlfriend during a difficult time, or if she was about to break up with him.

The carpet in the office somehow seemed older than the building. Volumes of leather-bound books completed the picture. This was an old-world law firm.

The man with slicked back grey hair sat behind the mahogany desk and spoke in warm and rich tones, no doubt honed through some time as a barrister in the past.

"Your father has left a bequest for each of you boys. The amount is equal, because, he says, he loved you equally. It's a quarter of a million dollars each. The remainder of his estate goes to your mother."

"There's only one thing further. He left an envelope for Aaron."

Aaron and Graham looked at each other.

Aaron could tell his sibling was thinking that despite the statement, his dad preferred his older brother, something they'd joked about throughout their lives, especially since their dad referred to Graham as his favourite second-born son.

"I have instructions to make sure he reads it now, alone." The lawyer gestured to the door. Graham grumbled as he left. His mother turned to Aaron as she walked out and told him she was going to give their car to Graham to drive home. She'd walk to the café next door in case he wanted to talk afterwards. His mother's hint of a smile contrasted her sad expression.

~

Aaron's eyes wandered round the room before settling on the letter in his hands. It was a plain manilla envelope, addressed in his father's distinctive scrawl 'to my favourite firstborn son'. Aaron peeled back the seal and extracted the letter inside. Again, it was printed on thick manilla paper. Aaron inhaled the faint, decayed scent of his father's aftershave and began to read.

My dear son.

I present this information to you with the hope it will serve you well. When it has been of use to you, pass it on to your brother or son(s) if you consider them worthy.

What follows is a method of making a woman fall in love with you. It's how I wooed your mother.

Aaron's forehead creased. Trickery? That didn't seem like the advice the wisest person he knew would give. Nor did it fit with how he'd viewed his parents' marriage growing up. They'd always seemed so in tune with each other. What would it mean if it was based on a lie?

Step one is to mimic your target's body language. This builds rapport between you as Duffy and Chartrand showed in 2015. This only works when you are motivated to form a bond. Intent is important.

Step two is to compliment the person. This makes them feel valued and shows an interest in them. You can also use NLP tricks such as "that's a 'loveme' dress/watch/wallet, where did you get it?" Make 'loveme' sound close to 'lovely'. You could also try 'dateme' in place of 'daily' when talking prior to asking for a date. The idea is that the brain will hear the correct phrasing, but then reprocess the sounds to the similar word since that interpretation makes more sense. The trick is that the brain will still trigger its mental processes associated with what was *actually* said, even if that version is not what the conversational response is based on. It helps if you follow the mixed-up word with a question, so the person focuses on answering that rather than interpreting the mixed-up word. Compliments can also boost the esteem of the person and associate you with that increase.

Step three is to make your first date something exciting like a horror movie, rock climbing, sports or dancing. This raises physiological arousal and can be misattributed as a positive emotional response to you, as per research by Aron and Dutton which showed people whose heart rates were elevated by walking across a scary bridge and met by an attractive researcher, were four times more likely to ask for a date than a control group who'd walked across a safe bridge. Other experiments have had similar results. The short version is that people will attribute their raised emotional state to the most pleasant thing in their immediate experience. In this case it was the researcher. So, if you take a date to something active or scary, they'll attribute their raised arousal to you rather than the situation, and thus feel like they have strong feelings for you.

Step four is to repeat this for the next few dates to take advantage of classical conditioning —the form of learning first described by Pavlov in regard to his dogs and subsequently used with humans by Watson. The TL/DR is the repeated increase in arousal when in the presence of the date, combined with misattribution will make it seem like romantic entanglement.

~

Aaron felt his sadness turning to anger. Had his father been nothing more than a conman?

Or was this some elaborate joke to make him angry so he would stop grieving? Aaron wouldn't put it past his father to try such a thing. But there was the nagging thought that the movie chosen by his father for his first date with Sophie was a horror movie, so it seemed like the steps were something his father believed in.

~

Step five is to hold hands as often as possible. A researcher, named Coan, showed holding hands reduces anxiety and cortisol levels. It switches off the threat response, making your date feel comfortable your presence—a great thing in the early development of a relationship. It's also known to trigger the release of oxytocin, the hormone which facilitates bonding behaviour. Hand holding can even be seen as a reward, thereby triggering operant conditioning processes which make your date feel an incentive to be with you.

Step six is a challenging one, not because of the difficulty of the act, but because of the restraint required. It is to hug often, but to hold the hug for at least twenty seconds. Grewen showed this causes the body to release oxytocin. The hard part is that the hug should be just that—no rubbing the back, or petting, or any sexual behaviour. Such a surge of the bonding hormone facilitates long term bonding and feelings of affection. The hug also makes the woman feel safe. You can hug without it being sexual and relax in the presence of each other. The beauty of these two steps is that you also experience the surge in hormones, and thus also gain the benefit of feeling closer to the person. It's also about you feeling real love for your partner. Following this with what is at least a 6 second French kiss will amplify the effect.

Step seven. Be an active listener. This makes your date feel heard, respected and valued. This helps generate positive feelings about you.

Step eight. Paraphrase what date has said back to them and/or tell them things they already know. As well as being part of active listening it makes the date feel as though they identify with you.

Step nine. Let the date 'win' at something. This triggers the dopamine-based reward pathways in the brain. Repeated stimulation of this pathway could lead to a classically conditioned sensation of winning when with date.

Use this knowledge wisely, my son.

I love you,

Dad.

~

Aaron wiped a tear from his cheek. He wasn't really sure why it was there. Was he mourning the loss of the father he thought he knew? The childhood memories of his parents seeming so in love being a lie? Or was it that this was the last piece of wisdom he'd get from his father?

Whichever reason it was, the longer Aaron sat in the office the angrier he felt. He put the letter back in the envelope and put it into his jacket pocket. He forcefully pushed the chair into the desk, then guiltily looked to the door when the resulting thud made him realise how much he'd overdone it. The look he got from the lawyer as he left, indicated he'd heard the commotion.

The fresh air did little to buoy Aaron's mood. He noticed people glance at him as they walked past. He wondered what they were making of his expression.

As he approached the cafe where the woman who had been the most important in his life; who had seemed half of a model for what a loving relationship should look like, his mind vacillated between what he'd just learnt and his own relationship. Anushka hadn't seemed happy recently, but then Aaron had been so caught up in work he hadn't paid her much attention. Maybe his dad's process was timely? Aaron wondered if he should talk to his mother now or give himself some time to reflect. In the end it was the half smile which made up his mind.

~

Aaron's mum's face made it clear she'd spent a lot of time crying over the last ten days. Without a word, Aaron sat opposite her at the little wooden table where she was nursing a chai tea.

"What's wrong, my son?"

His mum reached out to squuczc Aaron's

hand. Aaron sighed. Where to begin? His father wasn't the hero he thought he was. He'd duped his mother into their marriage.

"I…" Aaron slumped in his seat.

"Hmph. I must confess, I didn't think you'd take it this way. You look like you've just realised an action of yours injured a dog."

"No, it's not that…" Aaron frowned. "…You know what was in Dad's letter?"

"Of course. We had a partnership."

"But he manipulated you—"

"Your father confessed everything the day he proposed. He thought he'd been so clever in wooing me but felt that unless he told me how he'd engineered our early relationship, our marriage would be a sham. I listened to him attentively and told him I forgave him. He loved me and I loved him; that wasn't due to what he'd done but who he was."

"You knew…"

"Yes. My emotions were real and only encouraged by these steps. They weren't artificial. That's the key. The steps wouldn't work if there was no interest to begin with. They're simply a strategy to improve the potential of a long-term relationship. They can't force someone to love you. You can't force someone to love you."

"But they're manipulative."

"Maybe. But he didn't trick me into loving him."

"How can you say that given the steps he took?"

His mother smiled.

"It was his effort which was the most convincing thing. It was so clear he wanted to be with me, and he worked damn hard to make sure we got off to the strongest possible start. That was the kicker. If he was willing to put that much energy into forming our bond, that bode well for our future. That's one of the reasons I married him."

"I hadn't thought of it like that."

"Let me ask you a question. How much effort are you putting into your relationship with Anushka?"

Aaron studied the tabletop. "Not enough."

"Don't the steps teach you how important effort is?"

Aaron grimaced. "I guess so."

"May I see the paper?"

Aaron passed it to his mother, who took out a pen from her handbag.

"I see he left off step ten, but then that was something I added."

"What?" Aaron was floored. His mother had contributed to it too?

"It'll help you with Anushka. It's what I did to your father when I felt our relationship waning. It worked every time."

Aaron watched his mum write in the blank space. She drank the last of her tea and handed him the paper.

"You'll be fine. I love you, my favourite firstborn son."

Aaron read the paper. Step ten: Repeat steps one to nine. If it's meant to be, the relationship can be saved or strengthened by putting the effort into it.

With a rush Aaron realised much of what his dad had taught him about women over the years was probably what his dad had learnt from his mum. His mum was just as wise as his dad. No wonder they always seemed so loving.

"Woah," Aaron uttered.

"You know what? Despite all of your father's ability to read people and scientific knowledge he wasn't always the brightest."

"What do you mean?"

"He never knew what love actually was. Don't get me wrong, he felt it, but he never understood it…"

Aaron confusion show on his face.

"My poor boy. Love doesn't come from a dose of chemicals, nor any trickery with misheard words or misattributed emotion. Love is the recognition of a safe place in another person. Falling in love is the exploration of that space and finding the more you explore the more the boundaries recede."

Aaron felt his jaw open.

"What do all the steps your father identified have in common? They create feelings that even if times get scary, or even if they are good, no matter the circumstance you will be safe with and valued by that person. Look at them again and you'll see that idea of being a safe-place. That's what made me fall for your father, and why I'm devasted he's—"

Her voice caught in her throat. "—no longer with us. That's why reapplying your father's formula from time-to-time helps rekindle or keep the love alive… Let me ask you, how are you making Anushka feel safe?"

If his mother had slapped him as she spoke, her words could not have had more impact. Aaron looked absently around the room as his body found a few tears not yet shed. His erratic behaviour which had led to his arguments with Anushka would have made her feel a loss of confidence in his being there for her. No wonder she was withdrawing, and he felt like their relationship had stalled. They were no longer exploring the feeling of safety with each other. It was a hard truth to bear, but he knew he needed to accept it.

Aaron stood, thanked his mum, gave her a kiss on the cheek and started walking back to his car. For the first time that day he was looking forward to his date that night. Aaron smiled as he realised he wanted their relationship to succeed, and knew what to do about it.

References

Aron, A & Dutton, D (1974) Some Evidence for Heightened Sexual Attraction Under Conditions of High Anxiety *Journal of Personality and Social Psychology Vol. 30, 4*: 510-517.

Coan, JA, Schaefer, HS & Davidson, RJ (2006) Lending a hand: social regulation of the neural response to threat. *Psychological Science Dec;17(12)*:1032-9. DOI: 10.1111/j.1467-9280.2006.01832.x

Duffy, K & Chartrand, T (2015) The Extravert Advantage: How and When Extraverts Build Rapport with Other People
Psychological Science DOI: 10.1177/0956797615600890

Grewen, KM, Anderson, BJ, Girdler, SS & Light, KC (2003) Warm partner contact is related to lower cardiovascular reactivity. *Behavioural Medicine* Fall;29(3):123-30. https://doi.org/10.1080/0896428030959 6065

Schneiderman, I, Zagoory Sharon, O,

Leckman, J & Feldman, R (2012)
Oxytocin during the initial stages of
romantic attachment: Relations to
couples' interactive reciprocity
Psychoneuroendocrinology. Aug; 37(8): 1277–
1285.
https://www.ncbi.nlm.nih.gov/pmc/arti
cles/PMC3936960/

Angle of Repose
R. Andrew Russell

"What's this?" Nathan snatched the dog-eared paperback from my hand and stared at the title.

"Portony's Complaint. Why're you reading trash like that?"

"For my evening class."

"How does swearing and masturbation come into electronics?"

"It's for General Studies. You know, the subject that's supposed to broaden my education."

"Well, here's something else that'll do a better job." Nathan laid out a map of Southern Europe and indicated several red circles. "D'you know what these are?"

I pointed to one with a caption that I recognised. "Vesuvius, that's a volcano."

"Quite right, in fact they're all volcanos. I'm planning a trip to Italy to take a look at them as well as spending a few days in Rome and Pompei. Now you've got a job you should be able to afford a decent holiday. What d'you say to joining me?"

I'd only been overseas once before, on a school trip, and my cousin, who was a couple of years older, never missed the opportunity of presenting himself as more worldly. My first reaction was 'here we go again.' But at the same time, I was tempted. Stalling for time, I pointed to another of the red circles. "I've never heard of Vulcano."

"That'll be our first port of call, so to speak. It's a small volcanic island north of Sicily. D'you know anything about Roman mythology?"

As I shook my head, Nathan chuckled, pointed disparagingly to my novel and sighed.

"In Roman mythology, Vulcano's a chimney coming from the workshop of Vulcan, the Roman god of fire. As you might guess, the English word volcano comes from the island's name, 'Vulcano'. It last erupted in 1888, so we should be pretty safe."

Although I was enjoying my new life working while studying, I was captivated by the suggestion of a completely different adventure.

~

Apart from the Channel ferry, we travelled the entire distance from our home in England to Milazzo by a succession of trains. Of course, this predated the Channel Tunnel by many years. On the final leg of the rail journey I was amazed when the carriages of our train were loaded onto a ferry for the crossing between mainland Italy and Sicily. Milazzo, the end of our rail journey, is the main port for boats travelling to the Aeolian Isles, which include Vulcano. We stayed there overnight before boarding a hydrofoil to visit our first volcano. This unusual kind of vessel travels at twice the speed of the conventional ferry but sails with a peculiar lurching motion as it balances on underwater wings, reducing drag by lifting the hull clear of the water.

"That's our hotel." Nathan pointed out the whitewashed walls of a three-story building adjacent to the dock. As the hydrofoil curved into Vulcano's harbour it headed towards a berth directly opposite the Hotel Faraglione, our accommodation for five days.

"Great choice of hotel, Nathan. There's hardly any distance to carry our luggage."

He turned to point towards Vulcano's main cone. "Yes, and you can see the start of the track there, zig zagging up the side of the volcano."

~

During our first two days on the island, we visited popular tourist locations including climbing the main volcanic cone, circling its rim and descending into the crater. Vulcanello, two minor craters, separated from the main island by a narrow isthmus, provided a great view of the main cone.

"D'you know how volcanos get their distinctive shape?"

I didn't, but I was sure Nathan was about to tell me. He was passionate about everything to do with geology.

Gesticulating with his finger as we looked back at the main cone, he continued, "Volcanos are built up by the rain of ash particles which fall around their vents. Fragments of lava blown out of a central vent roll down the steeper parts of the cone until the slope becomes so gentle they stop. The inclination of the cone at this point is called the angle of repose. Here particles are resting stably, but only just."

To me, this made the whole volcanic cone sound quite precarious. "How does the cone keep its shape?"

"Over time, the ash hardens to form tuff, a kind of rock, but the profile stays about the same. Then, most things falling onto the sides of the cone simply slide down until they fall into the sea or add to the relatively level ground at the base of the cone."

Many of Vulcano's tourists visited the beach to cover themselves in its therapeutic mud or to swim. The beaches were black volcanic sand and the sea especially warm, heated by scalding, sulphurous bubbles rising from the seabed. The fumes made breathing a little difficult and after our first and only swim we found our towels had disintegrated, corroded by the caustic vapours. The acid also stripped the paint from our vacuum flask.

"I don't fancy spending any more time at the beach." I fully agreed with Nathan and as we walked back to our hotel he suggested something else to do the following day. "It would be great to walk around the base of the main cone to see it from all sides."

"Okay, we could ask at the hotel to see if they can give us directions."

Nathan shook his head. "No, they'd probably play another trick on us. Like they did last night. Fancy serving us plates of living sea snails, limpets and sea urchins."

Perhaps sensing my unease he continued, "What could possibly go wrong? We won't be doing a lot of climbing and can hardly get lost."

~

Our plan seemed so simple, we didn't think to leave a note at the hotel detailing how we intended to spend our day. Starting after breakfast we took our packed lunch and followed a well-worn track branching off from the tourist path leading to the top of the volcano. This trail seemed to head anticlockwise around the base of the volcanic cone. At least at the start, the ground was relatively flat. In the distance, we saw farm buildings and fenced off fields.

After a few minutes, we passed a young goatherd heading in the opposite direction, driving a herd of about twenty animals.

We waved a greeting, but the goatherd ignored us and concentrated on encouraging slower members of his herd with flicks of a thin wooden staff.

Nathan must have realised I still wasn't comfortable and tried to calm my fears. "Stop worrying will you. With the cone as our landmark, it's impossible to get lost."

We continued in uneasy silence until a fork in the road. I was expecting a moment's pause, but Nathan immediately chose the path to the left. "That's an easy choice," he said. "We just take the path heading closest to the direction we want to go."

This formula worked for several more junctions until we reached one where none of the choices led in the right direction.

"Perhaps this lack of tracks shows this isn't where people choose to go, and not even goats?"

Nathan didn't reply, but instead started his own track by wading through soft, uncompacted ground. Fine volcanic ash soon filled our shoes.

We estimated we were well over halfway round the cone when the flat, dusty terrain ended. To continue we had to step onto smooth volcanic rock angled steeply towards the sea.

"In some ways, this'll be better than ploughing through soft ground. At least we'll be able to stop emptying ash from our shoes."

I looked at the precarious angle of the ground and shook my head. "I know it's a long way to retrace our steps, but don't you think that'd be safer?"

Nathan couldn't stand to admit defeat. "We're both wearing our Doc Martens. You know they have an excellent grip on this volcanic rock. I don't think the sloping ground'll be a problem."

"But the lower slopes of the cone fall off sharply into the sea. It'll be very dangerous to get close to the edge where the sea's undercut the ground."

"No problem. We'll choose a direction that keeps us well away from the water."

Later, it became clear that there were major problems with the plan. When we took the track branching off right from the tourist path leading to the top of the volcano, we hadn't seen any tracks heading off left that would meet up with our current position. Unconsciously, we must have assumed there would be a connection. This had been a serious mistake.

Propelled by Nathan's boundless enthusiasm we continued, though not without difficulty. Looking ahead, all we could see was the steeply tilted slopes of the volcano and this made it difficult to keep our balance. Only the ocean's horizon and distant islands provided true orientation. By focusing on my feet and ignoring the rest of the surroundings, I managed to remain upright. However, I worried that any momentary lapse of attention might cause me to overbalance.

The next obstacle only became apparent little by little. Rain had cut channels into the soft volcanic rock and these crossed perpendicular to our chosen direction. As we continued the channels became deeper and wider, until Nathan became hidden from view when he was standing at the bottom of each of the gullies. He was scouting the way ahead and I didn't see or hear him fall. It was only when I looked into the next gully and saw him nursing a grazed and bloody elbow that I realised something had happened. Scrambling down to his level wasn't easy. I had to negotiate a few metres of crumbling rock to reach the bottom. Searching for a secure foothold, I dislodged a small boulder. Breaking free, it skipped and spun down the gully, gathering an avalanche of smaller stones. Eventually, they all splashed into the clear blue waters of the Tyrrhenian sea a couple of hundred metres below. The slope of the ground was greater than the angle of repose for the rocks and there had been nothing else to slow their fall. I'll never forget the vivid mental picture of what would have happened to me if I'd lost my footing. My path down the slope would have been similar. The inevitable injuries didn't bear thinking about. It was obvious our plans to circumnavigate the volcano had to change.

"We might have to change tack."

I agreed with Nathan's sentiment, but

even so I was sure he wouldn't agree to turn back. I tried to think of an alternative.

"We could climb up this gully and meet up with the path circling the crater."

Nathan looked sceptical. "The higher we go the greater the distance we could fall."

"Yes, but if we overbalance to the right or left the sides of the gully will save us. I'm sure it'll be safer, it'll certainly feel safer." My big worry, and one I didn't mention was the gully growing steeper, perhaps ending in an overhang. Both of these possibilities could block our way.

Nathan stepped to one side. "You go first, I've done my share of taking the lead."

To start with, the climb was relatively easy. Many rocks stuck out from the bed of the gully and provided convenient footholds. We used the sides for balance and to pull ourselves up. After a few tens of metres, we were making such good progress Nathan agreed that we could spare some time to rest. Each day, the hotel provided a bread roll with salami, an apple and a hard-boiled egg. We both wedged ourselves into crevices in the side of the gully and ate our food washed down with a cup of tea from our scorched vacuum flask. The odour of fresh bread and salami reminded me of how long we'd walked since breakfast.

The rumble of a powerful diesel engine rapidly increased in volume and as we watched, the afternoon hydrofoil curved round the island and headed for the harbour. At its closest, it was probably less than half a kilometre away.

My heart skipped a beat seeing help apparently so close at hand. Without fully considering what I hoped to achieve, I waved.

"No point." Nathan shook his head dismissively. "They'll never see you. Even if anyone's looking in our direction, we won't be seen. Our khaki shorts and green towelling shirts blend in too well with the browns and greys of the rocks."

"Well at least if they did see us, someone would know where we are."

Nathan seemed to take this as a criticism of his planning and changed the subject.

"We can't waste any more time chatting. We need to pack up the lunch things and continue the climb."

Carefully choosing each hand and foothold I pulled myself upwards.

"I'm sure this gully's becoming steeper."

Nathan grudgingly agreed. "You're probably right but we can't turn back now. Without eyes in the back of my head it'll be almost impossible to find footholds going backwards."

I felt as though our problems were compounding with only one possible result; absolute disaster.

Leading the way, I searched ahead by touch. I wanted to cling as close to the rock face as possible and didn't dare lift my head. It was impossible to see what was coming.

The handhold I was relying on crumbled and I grabbed for anything solid, but there was nothing. My uncoordinated lunges triggered a minor avalanche of pebbles. Nathan yelled out, "Watch what you're doing!" or something like that. Eventually, I realised my arm was searching empty space above flat ground. By carefully redistributing my weight I pulled myself up, out of the gully and onto level ground.

After helping Nathan climb up beside me, we both took in an otherworldly scene. Gently undulating slopes covered with grey gravel and angular rocks spread out as far as the eye could see. There were no paths, footprints or even plants. We found out this area is called Moon Lake and years later, when I saw images from the Apollo Moon landing, I realised how apt the name is.

Nathan turned and shook my hand. "This place is incredible. I'll never forget how you led the way up that vertical climb."

All I could think was how lucky we'd been to avoid the fate of rocks pushed beyond their angle of repose.

Fireflies
Erica Tippett

You lift your head ever so slightly. Crack! The shooting pain runs down the middle of your forehead and out the back of your neck. It's as if someone has hit you in the head with a hammer.

~

"The headaches will get worse, and body aches too," Dr Renda says.

You nod, focus moving in and out. It feels as if someone else is in the room with the doctor, not you.

"You can take paracetamol and ibuprofen. But don't use them nonstop for more than 5 days in a row."

Pain. The ache in your hip feels much worse than yesterday.

"Try to save them for when it's really bad. There are also stronger pain medications, but we try to use those sparingly these days. Too many people get addicted to them, and the side effects are awful."

Addiction. Maybe that's something worth trying. You never really have done anything that exciting. Always watching from the sidelines. Rarely joining in.

"Additionally, there are pain management programs I can refer you to." The doctor peers at you through grimy glasses.

The room feels stifling hot all the sudden. "Okay," you say. "I'd prefer to manage it with as little medication as possible." Of course you would. Addiction seems like too much trouble, anyway.

~

You rest your head back down. Dr Renda was not wrong. Breathe in, two, three, four, five. Breathe out, two, three, four, five, six, seven.

You roll over onto your back and gingerly open your eyes. The ceiling fan is of little comfort. Like a loyal pet, though, it's always there waiting when you wake. It asks nothing of you. No feeding or caring for. You roll onto your side using your left hand to push up to sitting.

There, that's not so bad.

You swing your legs over the side of the

bed. Your toes brush the floor. Leaning forward, you brace yourself. You did it, you're standing! You walk out of your bedroom and down the hall.

~

Thump, thump. Thump, thump, thump. You can't concentrate. You try to smile at Peta, but the concern in her eyes scares you. She looks as though she wants to ask you if you're really okay to do the class today. You've talked about this. Peta swallows audibly and moves on to the next student.

"That's looking really good," she says to Nadeem. Nadeem smiles his big, relaxed smile. It seems to put Peta at ease. You wish you had that kind of smile. You envy Nadeem. It must be so easy not being sick.

You shake your head at your pettiness and instantly regret it. Crack! The pain is intense. It takes your breath away. You cower back in your uncomfortable plastic chair and close your eyes. What a fool. You shouldn't have come to art class today.

~

Your phone dances across the bench, buzzing

like a bee. You reach for it and wonder if your head can take anymore today. It feels like it could crack right down the middle with the slightest provocation.

"Hello," you answer in your softest legible voice.

"Hello," comes the hushed response from Lorna. "Good and bad news." She doesn't pause for you to choose what order you'd prefer them in.

"The trip to Te Anau is on. But we can't get there until March."

Your mind reels, and the room spins. "What month are we in?"

"November."

"Oh." The light in the room feels bright. Blinding. You see greenish yellow spots in front of your eyes. "I'm not sure I'll be up to it in March," you say. Your stomach sinks. You're fairly certain you're not up to it now.

"I'll look for alternatives. But at least we've got that. Love you."

"Love you too."

"Bye." Lorna ends the call.

You put the phone back down, wishing

you had the energy to turn it off.

~

"I've been to Aotearoa, New Zealand twice," you explain to Julie, the nurse drip feeding your concoction of toxic chemicals today.

Julie nods, meticulously checking the line.

"Once to South Island for a wedding and once to the North. But I've never seen the glow worms in Te Anau. They're meant to be amazing." Tears form in your eyes. Your throat feels scratchy, but the words are begging to come out. "It's the last thing on my bucket list."

Julie is only the second person you've told that secret to after Lorna. She doesn't flinch. She finishes her work and pats you gently on the shoulder. "Well, I hope it all works out for you, darl." Her eyes are warm and kind when they briefly meet yours. "New Zealand is a lovely place. I'll be back in thirty minutes to check on this." She nods towards the drip, then shuffles off. Her no-nonsense black work shoes squeak on the shiny linoleum floor.

You look around the bright, sterile room. The chemicals are beginning their journey through your veins. In a matter of minutes, they will swirl around in your bloodstream and attack parts of your body, good and bad. You close your eyes and focus on your breath. The pounding of your head takes over and you count that instead. *One, two, three, four, five, six, seven, eight, nine, ten.*

~

You stare at the plate of food in front of you. Your stomach gurgles hungrily and you chase the broccoli slowly around the plate with your fork, with no intention of putting anything in your mouth. As you push the plate away, you think about how nice a cold blueberry smoothie would be right now. Crack! The pain shoots down from your head to your left big toe. The thought of the noisy blender makes you cringe. You reach for your phone, ignoring the pulse quickening thoughts of how you'll pay the credit card bill this month.

~

The Uber Eats driver bends over and places the paper bag on the doorstep. You see them peering at the 'don't knock' sign on the front door; a sideway glance at the taped-up doorbell. They take out their phone. Yours vibrates in your pocket. The delivery confirmation. You wait until the driver is back in their car before quietly opening the front door and collecting the drink. You sit on the couch and sip the cool liquid. The sweet scent of berries and milk waft pleasantly through the musty air. Your mouth ulcers protest a little. You wince, drinking slowly and staring into the distance.

~

The raven crows on the roof. Thump, thump, thump, thump. Your stomach is queasy. You don't dare take off the cute panda eye mask Lorna gave you. Not even to see ol' ceiling fan. You wish you could just drift off into the next realm. MRI scan day is one of those days you think you'd be better off dead. You curl up in the foetal position and bury your pounding head under the covers.

~

"You all set?"

You grit your teeth. "Yes."

"Remember, try not to move. If you need something urgently, put your hand up and we'll get you out. Okay?"

"Okay." You set your mouth in a straight line and close your eyes. Where is the calming stroll through the cool wetlands? The oversized headphones press on your right ear as though wanting to squash your head into the next magnificent clay creation from a potter's wheel.

You try to order your thoughts into something more conducive to survival in a buzzing metal tube. *The glow worms hang from their silks along the cave wall.* The bed slides further into the tunnel. Boom! You squeeze your eyes hard.

"Everything good in there?" The operator's voice seems like it's coming from miles away even though it's right in your ear.

You raise one shaky hand with a thumb up.

"Great, lie still now, arms down."

You rest your arms beside your spindly body.

"That's it. You're doing great."

"You are following the path that winds its way through Bennett's Wood." Finally, the meditation begins. "As you turn the first corner around to your left, you hear the crystal brook bubbling along not too far away."

You wish you could hear anything but the humming and buzzing of the dreaded machine.

"Before you get to the cool, clear waters, you pass through a tunnel of trees, their leaves thickly entwined on both sides of the narrow path. It feels like an entrance to another world."

You see the MRI tunnel clear in your mind's eye. What were you thinking, choosing this story? Your heartbeat pounds in your throat. Crack! The shooting pain is ferocious. You swallow hard. Think of something else!

"The little blue finch lands on a branch right in front of you. Its movements are fast as it sizes you up."

You try to imagine the bird but see only tunnels.

"Then it flits off, landing on a branch to the right, then flying through the trees and out of sight."

You have the strongest urge to flap your

arms and fly. To move your legs. You squeeze your eyes tighter in resistance.

"Count ten breaths. You can survive ten, easy. Then repeat it over and over for as long as you need." Lorna's smiling face dances before your eyes. Her soothing voice competes with the buzzing. How you love that woman. She has been your rock, your best friend. The only one who has stuck by you through all the pain.

One

Thump.

Two

Three

Thump. Thump. Thump.

Four

Thump.

Five

Six

Seven

Thump.

BUZZ.

Eight

"The creek flows faster here, gathering speed on its journey to the rocky edge, where it spills over, cascading in sheets down to the river below."

~

"Well done. We're all done here. Just a few more moments and you'll be out of the machine."

Your lips curl into a smile and you move your hands and arms just a little. You wiggle your toes and make tiny circles with your ankles. The pain in your head throbs in the background. Freedom is so close. The intense feeling of liberation washes over you. For the first time in over a month, you feel something akin to joy.

~

Lorna looks into your eyes. "You don't have to do this. I've got it."

"I know," you say, gritting your teeth. Your hands feel slimy from the soap. "But I want to. I really want to. I want to feel normal; useful."

"We could go for a walk. That's normal; healthy." She looks at your face.

You feel you're scowling but aren't sure how to stop.

"You know what I mean. A slow walk might be…" Lorna looks down at her hands.

You smile, but it's hollow. "When did we become like an old married couple?"

Lorna's face melts. Tears spring to her eyes. "I'm so sorry, but I can't. Not today. Do what you want. I just… can't." She flees the room.

You see how careful she is with the front door, closing it as though it's made from the world's most precious crystal. You wonder how much she wants to slam it. To make noise. Shout at you. Scream at the world and its cruelty.

You return to scrubbing the cupboards. This place has to look it's best to have a hope in fetching the price you need to pay all the debt. All those medical bills. The realtor was not at all comforting. Then there's the trip to Aotearoa. You chuckle at the thought. It all seems like a fantasy. Someone else's dream that's becoming your nightmare. You swallow the dread down with water, a handful of paracetamol and ibuprofen.

~

"Welcome all to the auction of 185 Briars Lane," the Auctioneer bellows. "We are ready to get underway here on this beautiful sunny day. And what a property it is."

You squeeze Lorna's hand. "I'm having second thoughts about being here," you admit.

Lorna looks at you. "Want to go sit in the garden? We'll still probably be able to hear him, though. He sure is loud!"

Thump, thump, thump. You nod and follow Lorna through the door. The pristine cupboards blur as you stumble through the kitchen. The sparkling glass seems to mock you as you walk out into the garden.

"I'm surprised they didn't hold the auction out here," Lorna says. She admires the neatly trimmed plants in their planter boxes. "You did such a marvellous job cleaning the place up."

You beam. "Thanks. I'm so happy with how it turned out." Crack! The pain shoots straight down your spine and you reach out and grab the back of a chair.

Lorna notices and pulls the chair out so you can sit.

Once settled, you lean forward. "Makes me wish I'd never let it get so messy."

"It's great to see all the people here."

You blink slowly. "Yeah. Let's hope there are some real buyers among them."

Lorna sits down next to you.

You marvel at how nice it is to sit in the garden and have a conversation that's not medical. So rare these days. "You look lovely today. I really like that dress on you."

Lorna blushes. She takes your hand. "Thanks. It's really nice to hear that."

"At five hundred and fifty thousand, going once!" The auctioneer's words interrupt the peace of the garden.

Lorna looks at you.

"It's not enough," you say with despair.

She wraps you in a hug and you feel the tension melt from your body. The tears fall and you are powerless against them. Burying your face in Lorna's shoulder, you hear nothing but the thumping of her heart. Or is it your head?

~

Lorna gently nudges you and you realise you must have drifted off.

The taste in your mouth is bitter and you swallow uncomfortably. "What did it sell for?"

"It sounded like six ten."

Your eyes bulge. You look at Lorna's face. There are tear tracks marking her cheeks.

"It got that high?" The pounding fades into the background.

"Yeah, I think so." She looks away from you.

"Should we go inside?" You look at your shaky hands. "Oh, I feel all jittery."

"Might as well go in." Lorna stands and walks to the door. "I wouldn't mind a cuppa. Would you like anything?"

"Just some water. I'll get it once you've boiled the kettle."

"I'll give you the signal," Lorna says.

~

The auctioneer strides into the kitchen. "There you are."

You rise from the table.

"Six hundred and ten thousand. Great result. Very keen buyer. Congratulations. Good outcome. Very good. Come and sign the paperwork."

You follow the auctioneer into the lounge room and perch on the sofa.

"Sign here, and here."

Your hand shakes. You do your best to recreate your legal signature. It looks a bit off.

"And here. And here." He looks at the paper. "All done."

"Thank you," you say, shaking his outstretched hand.

"You're welcome. Well, I best be off." The auctioneer gathers up the papers and puts them in his shiny briefcase. "Got two more auctions today."

You nod slightly and he breezes out of the room.

~

The doctor calls your name and you stand, following her into the consulting room. She gestures for you to sit.

You are on the other side of the large wooden desk. Crack! The pain rushes into your lower back. The room is stuffy, and you start to perspire. You wonder how much bad news Dr Renda has had to deliver over this desk. Your underarms feel awfully wet.

"I have the results of your MRI."

You brace yourself.

"No Lorna today?"

You shake your head softly. "She couldn't get off work."

"That's a shame. Sandra, it's not good news I'm afraid."

Despite your best efforts, tears spring to your eyes.

"The cancer has spread again. There are new nodes in your lungs and stomach. The chemo isn't working any longer."

All you can manage is, "Oh."

"We've talked about options before. Other treatments. I know you had financial constraints."

"I sold my house. It settles next month."

"Well that's great news. Do you want to look at the new drug I was telling you about? The one that's fifty thousand per 28-day treatment?"

The room swirls. "I… um. Maybe. I need to think about it. Discuss it with Lorna."

"Of course. Do you still have the information or should I give it to you again?"

"Ah, if you could give it to me again. I'm not sure where it is in all the boxes." You look down at your hands.

"Sure. Here we are." The doctor reaches for a folder and flicks through a few pages. She pulls out a pamphlet from its protective plastic sleeve and passes it across the table.

"And if I don't go ahead with the new treatment?"

"I would suggest stopping the current course of chemotherapy regardless. It's not making anything better and the side effects have been very unpleasant for you. If you don't choose to try the new treatment you'll need stronger pain relief. I'll update your pain management plan."

"And how long do you think I've got?"

"Two to three months, at best."

You grit your teeth. "So, until around February?"

"Yes. I'm sorry, Sandra."

"And the treatment could buy me how much time?"

"It's hard to say of course, but probably six months or more. If it's successful it could send you into remission. Then you would have years, possibly many.”

You blink slowly.

“I know it’s a lot to take in. Go and read the information carefully and talk it over with Lorna.”

“Okay. Yes. Thank you.”

“Come back and see me next week and we’ll make whatever arrangements we need.”

You nod and stand. You wish you had the energy to run out of the room, down the street, out of this place altogether. “Thanks,” you mumble again, and shuffle out of the room.

~

You wait nervously for Lorna. She’s late. You feel panic rise from your gut. What if she’s been hurt? What if she’s dead? She could have had an accident on her way here.

You wish you had made plans to meet at her place, instead of the lakeside café. At least it’s quiet outside due to the unusually cool weather. You look at the crowded tables inside, thankful for the heavy door that contains the noise and bustle.

You exhale loudly at the sight of Lorna in

her red coat, head stooped forward, bracing against the chilly wind. Your relief turns to dread at the thought of sharing your news.

"So sorry I'm late. I've had a hell of a week. So glad it's nearly the weekend."

You give her a quick hug. "That's okay. I've been watching the ducks," you lie.

"Are you hungry? I'm starving. I'll go order."

You shake your head. "Maybe just a drink for me. A milkshake. Ah, vanilla, thanks."

"Sure, be right back."

Lorna returns after a few minutes, carrying table number 23. "It's so busy in there."

She sits across from you.

"Oh, this chair is freezing." Lorna gathers her coat so it's under her legs.

You swallow. "This is hard for me to say, so I'm just going to say it all at once. I got my MRI results, bad news I'm afraid. The cancer has spread." Lorna's face drops. You look down at the table and fix your gaze on a tomato sauce stain. "It's not responding to the treatment anymore. There is one other option.

It's the really expensive drug we talked about a while ago. The one that costs fifty thousand per month. It could buy me six months or more. Otherwise, I've got until February or so." Crack! The pain shoots into your right wrist. You close your eyes momentarily, then look up.

Lorna takes your hand across the table.

You grit your teeth so as not to flinch.

"You're going to try the new treatment, right? I know it's a lot of money, but with the house sale, you've got at least enough for one month's worth, straight up?"

"I'm not sure one month will be enough. What if it doesn't work?"

Lorna squeezes your hand. "You won't have to worry about money then."

"But what about funeral costs?"

Lorna swallows. Her face looks grey, sallow.

The knot in your stomach tightens. "And what if it does work? Then I'll be alive but destitute."

The café door opens. A server carries a tray with a mug of coffee, a tall silver milkshake cup and a large slice of lemon meringue pie on a plate. She dumps the contents on the table.

"Thanks," Lorna squeaks.

You can't look at either of them, so fix your sights on the milkshake cup. Your forlorn reflection bounces back at you. You turn away and look at the brown lake.

"You have to try," Lorna says. Her voice cracks. "Please. For me."

~

Lorna pulls your hand gently. "Come on, just a bit further."

The sun is low in the December sky. It must be pushing 8pm. The warm breeze dances across your bare arms.

"I know it's not as exciting as Te Anau, but it's amazing to find what's in your own backyard."

Thump. "What? Is that why you brought me to the Blue Mountains?" Thump. Thump. Thump. Suddenly, your legs feel like jelly. "Are there glow worms out here? I thought you only found them in caves."

"Not exactly. I mean, yes, you only find glow worms in caves. And yes, there are glow worms in the Blue Mountains. But that's not what we're looking for tonight. Hopefully, we'll see glow worms tomorrow, or the day after."

Your mind races as you walk along the deserted road. Thump. Thump. It hurts to think. It hurts to walk. Everything hurts. Thump. Thump. Your head pounds in time with your slow steps.

Lorna pauses, looking down at her map. Then she nods her head. "This will do it." She turns onto a narrow path leading into the woods. "Only a few metres more. I promise. Here. This is the spot."

Lorna drops your hand and shrugs off her backpack. She pulls out a picnic blanket and a cushion. There's not much space in between the trees, but she sets up a comfortable seating area for two. "Sit down," she directs.

"Thanks," you say, finding your way gingerly onto the seat. The light is fading fast now.

Lorna retrieves a small bottle of sparkling wine from the bag. "I didn't have space for glasses, so we'll just have to sip it from the bottle." She pops the cork and passes it to me.

"To living life, while you can," you say, raising the bottle into the air. You take a sip. The bubbles dance on your tongue. Your mouth burns. You pass the bottle to Lorna.

"Cheers," she says and takes a big gulp. She doesn't look at you when she eventually passes the bottle back.

It's dark by the time you finish the bottle. You've had maybe three sips. All for show. For Lorna. The sounds of insects fill the air. It's as if you can feel the reverberations, the air bouncing around you off cicadas' wings. An unusual peacefulness descends on you. The cooler night air makes your arms prickle with goosebumps. You rub your arms gently.

Lorna notices. "Here, take my jacket. I'm still warm from the walk. You know me, always warm."

She passes the jacket to you, and you drape it over your shoulders.

You sit for a long time, not talking. You like how easy it is to sit with Lorna in comfortable silence. Closing your eyes, you feel like you're floating, drifting off along a cool current.

"Look! I see one," Lorna says in an excited whisper.

You flutter your eyes open and return to the night in the woods. There's a bright flash. Then another, to the right of the first, then two more to the left. "Wow," you say, trying to keep your voice low.

The flashes seem to form a pattern. You see one close by on a long blade of grass. It's close enough that you can just make out an outline of the beetle's body extending from its luminescent bottom section. But only for a few seconds.

Tears well in your eyes. They track down your cheeks over well-worn paths and drip off your chin onto Lorna's jacket. These tears are different, though. Tears of joy and wonder at the beauty of this world. The world you will soon leave behind. You can feel it. Your time is ending. You feel it in the space where there was dread and anger and fear. It's different now. It feels inevitable. Meant to be.

Like a flash of light, ending in darkness.

Like the fireflies.

Poetry

Love...
Robert Eisler

How will I
Remember…
Your name Your words
Your smile?
Is who you are now Who you were
Who you'll be in a while?

Love they say's eternal Not whimsy -
Here
There

gone… Flight of fancy Fleeting, sylph-like
Vaguely hummed old song

Are we
Not
Merely…
Love's vessels…
Flowers deep of night Incandescent radiant
Each of us
Swift flight…

Glorious…
Moments only… Ethereal consciousness?
Love, are we not Dreams…
And
As dreams, With love, Blessed?
No.
In love
We are love's sunshine
Sweet music, love's delights… Whirling dance
Twining fates
Laughter beauty heights…
Of passion to transcend
Space time eternity
In love
You ARE love
As am
I love…
You are
Part
Of me…

And so, love
Will we ALWAYS be
Love flowing of seas Universes…
Of ether…

That IS
Love…
You and
Me

Love has ALWAYS been… As, love, so have
we too
We will not REMEMBER love
As love IS…
Me and you…
And as we live
Of love
ARE love
We, love
Shall NEVER fret…

For you will not
Remember…

And I…

Never…
Will…
Forget

I Will Never Forget

Robert Eisler

The wonder-struck buffoon
Called Harold (Blankie) Arbuthnot
Who flew up to the moon Upon a magic carpet
Powered by bull-rushes They made a MOVIE
out of it You should have seen the rushes!

Harold was AMAZING
Worthy of great rhymes
The reason why I liked the guy?
He DANCED all of the time! Danced vast
forests
Through green meadows
By the rolling seas
Through the flowing ocean deeps
Harold LOVED to meet All the mer-folk
living
In their shining mer-folk caves Where they had
such MARVELLOUS times Underneath the
waves!

He danced on golden seashores

He danced upon great plains
Through vast deserts, sleet and snow Sunshine
pouring rain
And EVERYWHERE dear Harold danced
Life bloomed verdant green
And lustrous, like a rainbow Sweetest colours
ever seen!

One fine day dear Harold Blankie
Danced into the SKY We never saw Harold
AGAIN
I REALLY don't know WHY
I was THERE when Harold
Disappeared into the blue
(Yes! All of this DID happen…
I SWEAR the whole thing's true!…)

He shouted down a message
As he rose into the air Flying from to a
mystery…
No one quite knows where,
"I'll never forget a one of you!" he cried "You
are my greatest treats!
EVERY creature on this Earth
Danced me off my feet I've only ONE

important message It's of these blue skies
above:

DANCE! Just DANCE!
ALL you're worth
And,
PLEASE…

Make
HEAPS
Of
Love!"

I Will Never Forget
Katharina Fares

A hospital bombed
killing countless patients
the sick and wounded
Old people and children

Worse is to come
soldiers move in
two doctors are executed
scores of others arrested
taken away
to an unknown location

Empty rooms
stripped bare of beds
medical equipment
and pain medication

Rows of injured children
lying on the dirty tiled floor
covered with dust and blood

The care workers
who are still there
are wetting a cloth
in a kidney shaped dish
cleaning gaping wounds
and soot covered faces

The water is cut off
The electricity is cut off
bringing certain death
to premature babies
and all patients on
life saving equipment

Doctors
who haven't been taken away
must amputate
shattered limbs or
body parts with gangrene
by the light of torches
or mobile phones
without anaesthetic and
without pain medication

Source: Doctors without Borders

I Will Never Forget #2
Katharina Fares

I will never forget
A courageous little girl called Hind
perhaps seven years old
No one survived who
could confirm her age

Her hometown
is relentlessly bombed
ground troops move in
creating fear and chaos

People who have a car or a cart
are fleeing from danger
Hind can't fit into her family's car
but she follows with her uncle

Stunned
by witnessing her family
going up in flames
hearing the screams
of her parents and siblings

Her uncle moves on
speeding away
from imminent death
but there is no escape

They hear artillery fire near by
a hail of bullets rains down
the car stops
Shocked

Hind realizes she is still alive
Surrounded by silence
by deadly silence
everyone around her
is covered in blood
She calls the name of each
of the five men in the car
not one answers

Dazed
she touches one after another
not one moves
she understands
they are all dead

Terrified
by the descending darkness
she huddles against her dead cousin
seeking comfort
but feels it will never come

Exhausted
she crouches down
and falls asleep
at the floor of the car

Awoken by the song of a bird
she looks up at a clear blue sky
but then she remembers
the horror surrounding her

Fear paralyses her thoughts
makes her limbs feel heavy
she calls out
help help please help me
there is no reply

Allah I beg you
don't leave me alone
please help me

thoughts are racing
through her mind what can I do how can I get
help

Rifling through the belongings of the dead
she finds a mobile phone
perhaps more than one
she dials the number of the Red Crescent
and keeps calling and calling and calling
until finally she is heard

Please please come and get me
I'm alone in a car on the road to the south
I'm scared
my uncle and my cousins are all dead
I'm alone I'm scared
please come and get me

An Ambulance with two paramedics
is sent to rescue Hind
after a day the base loses contact
with them and with Hind
Searching
they find the burned-out ambulance
and the bodies of the two paramedics

Days later they find Hind's body
with a gunshot wound
still in the car
between the five male bodies

I Will Never Forget #3

Katharina Fares

A little toddler-girl
unsteadily swaying
on her tiny feet
Surrounded
by the dust of falling debris
stumbling through devastation
as far as she can see

Searching
the mountain of rubble
which seconds before
had been home
Calling
Mama I'm here Mama come
Baba Baba come and get me
Mama I'm afraid

The sound of falling bombs
mingles
with cracks of thunder
and pelting rain
Mama I'm cold I'm cold

She sees
a small cat sheltering
under a fallen concrete slab
she crawls in beside the cat
holding her close
stroking her wet fur
whispering
don't be afraid I'm here

I Will Never Forget #4
Katharina Fares

An injured boy
less than ten years old
ignoring a Paramedic
who wants to tend his wound

Standing immobile
with paralysing fear
where is my mother
where is my brother
he cries out again and again

A river of tears flooding
his blackened face
where is my little brother
where is he where is he
I couldn't protect him

He looks up he looks down
searching the ruins around him
there he is under that car
beside our destroyed house
blood runs out of his mouth

I Will Never Forget #5

Katharina Fares

The young man who
overnight turned old

His hair is singed off
holes are burned into his coat
his face is covered with dust

He stares at the rubble
which had been his home
had sheltered his loved ones

Now he doesn't know
who is alive who is dead

He sees
an arm he sees a leg
an unrecognisable head
he sees the dead
who have no names

He searches

the ruins for body parts
he puts them together
assembling a boy or a girl

giving them back their names

I Will Never Forget Haiku

Katharina Fares

Hoping and waiting
Searching as long as life lasts
For one always loved

Pictures of children
Damaged by smoke and blood
Kept at mothers' hearts

The only proof they had
Of one cherished and loved
Traded for new hope

Pinned to a wall
Torn images of children
Who were lost at war

Waiting by the Phone
By Sung-Ju Suya Lee

Disconnected?
Silence is the loudest sound
When you wait by the phone.
One minute, your mouth waters
As if the Hoover Dam cracked
Between your teeth with no bite.
The next, it's dry as the thoughts
In a once-in-a-century drought.
Dying.
Silence dares you to breathe
In the middle of the Outback
Where there is no water pump
To fill your soul with lies and hope.
Silence chips away at grandeurs,
At delusions of fireworks of fame.
Swipes in all directions, but
The next step forward.
Lost.
Your feet soak into Quicksand
Drowning in Disneyland's corpus
Of wishes, dreams, and fantasies.

Silence mocks visualization boards
As much as The Law of Attraction
Traps you with a bear paw trap
Twisted by Feng Shui's rearrangement
Disorder of reality and factuality.
No joke laughs at the bottom line of
Common sense at the bank of the
Lucky.
Silence makes success wait
Outside the door that's bolted
With a black hole named Void.
No key works as Silence tosses
Any effort spinning and sinking
Into Medusa's soulless pupils.
Your brain burns, your fingers
Bleed, your heart bursts more
Than the Big Bang.
No ring. No ping. No ding.
Line. Is. Dead.

Unplug the phone.

Ode to Struggling Writers
By Sung-Ju Suya Lee

Hello world. We kowtow to the mighty literary lotto.

Wishing upon a star in Hollywood's shadow.

Koala bears take it slow. Watch the world go and flow.

Kangaroos jump like a pro. Throw woes like a yo-yo.

Fellowships bestow a combo, highlight low to glow...

Help each other with writing mojo,

Wipe our brows, grease our elbows with ammo,

To show off our creative judo with gusto.

Play with words and thoughts like a banjo.

Re-arrange them on the page like Van Gogh.

The Monash Writers Group guides us like dynamos.

Our muses' accountability is a soul Tae Kwon Do.

Our annual anthologies ups our status quo.

Spit out the self-annihilating tobacco.

Torpedo those self-doubts, bounce on our bongo.

Dig below the negative, borrow through the writing foe.

Undergo a transformation, fly on a story UFO.

Radio in our dreams, improvement is our manifesto.

Pile up our portfolios, minutes to words ratio.

Ha, ha! End of year reflections. Excuses have escaped.

My to do-list and resolutions already pear-shaped.

A Young Storyteller

By Sung-Ju Suya Lee

Who sits on the small shoulders of a young storyteller?

Muses from fairy tales and fables. Muses from TV cartons and movies with animals. Muses from vinyl records singing for you to clap your hands. Muses from bullies who pull your hair. Muses from teachers who think you are invisible. Muses from classmates who never pick you for their team. Muses from the Valentine's cards never addressed to you. Muses from the racist taunts that make you cry. Muses from beatings from the ones who were supposed to love you the most. Muses from blackened hearts who could never show you the light.

The Bride

Dilys Smith

As a ray of light she first appeared,
Coming slowly with a smile,
That held such warmth for all who looked,
That the waiting seemed worthwhile.

Her gown was white and billowing,
And her veil so mistily fell,
That they had to strain to see the smile
On the face they knew so well.

Then, when the veil was lifted,
And her smile shone forth so bright,
There was happiness on every face,
And every heart felt light.

After days and nights of heavy fog,
Of biting cold, and muscles aching,
For her the sky had turned to blue,
A perfect setting making.

And there, in all her splendour,

With her smile so warm and gay,
The Sun shone over Melbourne
Like a bride on her wedding day.

Japan

Dilys Smith

It was a 9.8 earthquake,
Off the East Coast of Japan,
That started the greatest Tsunami
Overflowing the defences of man.

It cared not for people or places,
Cars, boats, buildings or land,
It tore over all in its pathway,
So much power was at its command.

Houses went down as it ploughed through,
Railways torn up and then stood,
Making rail lines look just like fences
With the rails upright holding the wood.

Large houses were pushed to their limit
Till upturned, they floated away
Along with cars, houses and debris,
Over everything else on the way.

It savagely took on the airport,

Invaded the green fields and crops,
And ravaged the whole countryside,
As it ruthlessly pulled out all stops.

Thousands of people have perished
Who believed they were safe in their homes.
No one knows who will be safe though,
Once an earthquake tsunami comes.

Memoir

I'll Never Forget

Sakuntala Gananathan

My memory is full of unforgettable instances throughout my life. Most of them happy, surprising, while some were heartbreaking. What about the incident that took place last year?

I had arrived at that town three months earlier and would commute to work by train. I would leave for work early in the morning and return near dinner time, such that I had no time to get to know even my immediate neighbours. The only friend I had was Maureen who lived in the next street.

I had just returned from work and after a quick wash got dressed up. I wore a red and green evening gown because I had a matching necklace of emeralds and pair of earrings also of emeralds. As I was applying makeup, Maureen phoned me.

Alas she was down with the flu and couldn't attend the wedding. "Eliza dear, remember the directions I gave you last week.

The church is at the corner where the road branches off across the bridge. You are new to this place and I am particular you don't take a wrong turn. And don't travel by bus, for goodness's sake!"

I thanked her and switched off the phone. How is she to know that I don't have much money to take fancy rides in taxis when my finances are so low?

Snatching my handbag, I rushed out to take the express bus at the end of our street. But as luck would have it, the bus took off as though to tease me.

However not all were lost. There was a cab parked about 15 yards away. The driver put his head out and called out, "Miss, please jump in and I'll take you to your destination faster than that cursed bus you just missed."

I thanked him and got in the cab, after which I gave him the direction to the church.

"But Miss, are you sure that's the church you wish to go to? There's another church…"

The next five minutes we got into an argument and I had to rudely tell him off that if he didn't stop harassing me, I would get down and take another taxi.

That made him shut up and he dropped me at the church I had directed him to. There were numerous cars parked in the driveway. I paid his fare and got off in a hurry.

I made sure my gown wasn't crushed.

As I entered the doorway, they were singing hymns. The hall was full of people and a gentleman pointed out to a vacant seat to me on the extreme right just near the entrance. I ignored him and walked down further so that the crowd could see me in all my glory. Not surprisingly the crowd, especially the ladies, craned their necks to look at me.

There was a vacant seat half way down, but a lady had left her handbag on that. I said, "May I…?"

She was surprised but put her handbag …a plain looking grey bag on her lap.

I thanked her and sat down. All eyes were turned on me. There were hushed whispers and giggles such that the priest had to order, "Silence please!"

He then started his sermon and I thought I would die of shame. Without a moment to lose, I got up and ran back to the Church entrance.

How did I come to the wrong venue I wondered.

A cab driver tooted the horn and it was a god send. I rushed up to the cab and got in.

"I told you Miss, that you were going to the wrong church. There is a wedding taking place further down the road. I'll take you …"

I wouldn't let him finish his sentence but ordered, "Take me back to my home, would you?" and gave him my address.

I switched off my mobile phone in the days and weeks immediately following, because I didn't wish to hear, "Eliza are you nuts to attend a funeral dressed up like a clown?"

I'll Never Forget: Summers in Melbourne
Marlene Laurent

Every Summer, I went to the Australian Open Tennis. Apart from the excitement of seeing the players and watching them perform their very best, I always felt, although we were strangers, we were a community united by our love of tennis.

Standing at the entrance to Rod Laver Arena, waiting for Shunji to arrive, I remembered when I first took him to the Men's Final. It was the 1990s and Shunji was a Japanese intern living with us.

The school I was working at taught Japanese as a LOTE subject (Language Other than English). I always thought this a strange choice because the school was multi-cultural and had 45 different nationalities. For the majority of students English was their second language. Why would we confuse them even more by introducing them to a third language? Anyway, we applied for a Japanese intern. The deal was they'd help out teaching the culture and language and in exchange we'd host them. They'd live with an Aussie family and learn English.

We were successful and, as I had put my name down to be a host family, Shunji came to live with us and came to work with me. He became a member of the family and we had lots of laughs from day one when he arrived on his motorbike in his ski gear, even though it was a hot summer Melbourne day! Thinking we'd do the right thing we took him to Aussie events, such as the AFL at the mighty MCG. He'd insisted on wearing his snow gear. Suddenly the sun was shining. One beer later he had fallen asleep. When he woke up, he was fascinated by the behaviour of the crowd. "Baaall!" they all shouted

"Free kick," the guy in front called out!

"Coll…ing…wood," the crowd cheered.

"What does that mean?" he kept asking all day! We realised he wasn't really interested in the footy!

However, when we went to the tennis, he really enjoyed it. As the temperature reached

35 degrees Celsius, he decided to take his t-shirt off and get a suntan. "I be like an Aussie," he said.

"You'll get sunburnt, at least put on some sunscreen and wear a hat," I replied.

"Didn't bring one."

I tried to talk him into buying one that he could have as a memento, but he wasn't interested.

On the way home, Shunji wasn't feeling well, displaying symptoms of sunstroke. A trip to the doctor and an application of yoghurt to ease the pain, Shunji grabbed his dictionary, looking up the word sunburnt. "I'll use sunblock and wear a t-shirt next time," he winced. I just smiled and said nothing.

Despite this experience he was hooked on going to the Australian Open.

Eventually we said goodbye and Shunji returned to Japan. He came back to Australia for the tennis whenever he could and we kept in touch, saying he was always welcome to stay at our home in Melbourne.

I was jolted back to reality as I heard a familiar voice, "Gidday mate!"

It was my friend from Japan who had just flown in for the Australian Open.

"Oh, hi Shunji, great to see you again. Thanks for the ticket."

"No worries, mate."

"So where are our seats?"

"Third row from the front near the entrance where the players come onto the court."

"You're kidding me. That's fantastic."

Sitting in the stadium, the air was electric as fans anticipated the players' arrival on centre court. Then Shunji's phone rang.

"Moshi Moshi," he said laughing. "It's my friend from Fitzroy; he wants me to meet him for lunch."

"No way, you can't go now, you'll miss the final."

"Yes, I want to catch up with my Aussie friends."

"Ok give me your ticket and I'll give it to someone."

Wandering outside the stadium to where fans were sitting on the grass watching the big screen, I looked for someone on their own.

Weaving my way through the crowd I spotted a guy sitting by himself.

"Hi, would you like to see the Men's Final today?" I asked, showing him the ticket.

"Yes, but how much do you want for it?"

"It's free, only downside is you get to sit next to me."

He laughed, "That's not a problem. I'll shout you lunch," he offered. I enjoyed the chicken and we shared the chips.

"How did you end up with a spare ticket for the Men's Final? It's really difficult to get tickets anytime let alone on the day." I explained the situation.

"Really hard to believe that story but I know you have no reason to make it up."

I can't remember who played and who won but I'm guessing Pete Sampras or Jim Courier as that was their era.

~

I usually drove to Riversdale Road and caught the free tram to Rod Laver as it is quite convenient and because some night matches don't finish until late. Like the time Lleyton Hewett's match went until 3am. The taxis were lined up outside as the last train left at midnight. Agonising over the dilemma to go or stay I ended up staying. The taxi driver was annoyed when I said, "Hawthorn, please!"

I knew the fare was only $10 and I could drive myself home from there. As I had two tickets, I asked my daughter if she came to the tennis who would she like to see.

"Goran Ivanisevic," she replied.

"Really? He's a bit crazy."

"Yes, that's why I like him."

She came with me to the 3am match because Goran Ivanisevic was playing Lleyton Hewitt.

"You can't barrack for Goran; you have to barrack for the Aussie."

"Really, Mum? OK."

Goran won so she was quietly happy!

~

Kooyong provided an opportunity for the players to get in some match practice. My tennis club was issued with tickets for this event so I said I'd be interested in going. Seating is limited so you get to see the players up close and personal. It's quite a different feel from Rod Laver Arena.

Luckily the day I went Roger Federer was playing. He put on a perfect performance. What a shame, I thought, as he won in straight sets. I would have liked to see more of him. After Federer had finished his game, he walked down the path to the club house. I rushed to get in the front row behind the fence and watch him heading towards me. A young fan called out "Roger, I love you. Will you marry me?"

The crowd was laughing, as was Roger. He struck me as a genuinely nice person. Of course, I already knew he was one of the best. Although my hand was shaking my finger was pressing quickly as I took shots of him with my phone. He was very popular and is still my favourite player.

~

It was 2004 and I was at work when I noticed an email from my friend from Perth. Oh she's contacting me to ask if I'm going to the Boxing Day test, I thought, because we were both cricket tragics. We went to Lords for the Aussie v England match. Surprisingly she was asking if I'd be interested in going to the finals of the Australian Open 2005. She was coming to Melbourne for the Boxing Day test and thinking about staying on for the tennis. She knew I went every year and had suggested to her to join me sometime. After checking the cost online, I was tempted to say, "You're kidding me," but thought, "Why not?"

It was the beginning of the era of the dominance of the big three, Federer, Nadal and Djokovic. Our best Aussie player was Lleyton Hewitt. It could be interesting finals. What if Lleyton won? It'd be great to see that, I thought. So I said yes and bought tickets for the finals.

On Australia Day, we met at the stadium, and she handed me a pair of sunglasses with boxing kangaroo lenses. She was wearing a pair with the Australian flag on them.

"Can you see out of them?"

"Try them on and see."

"Where did you get them?"

"I bought them to sell at the tennis. Thought they'd be popular and I could make some money to pay for my tickets."

"You're not expecting me to sell these are you?'

"Only if you want to. It's easy, just watch."

Approaching a couple in the coffee queue she chatted to them. "Hi, how are you today?"

"We're fine thanks. I like your glasses, they're neat."

"I have a pair for sale. $10 if you're interested."

Needless to say, she sold one of each. That day we ended up on the news wearing our sunglasses and singing the National anthem, because it was Australia Day.

Marat Safin played Lleyton Hewitt in the Men's Final. It was a four setter. Lleyton, taking the first 6.1. We were so excited! The rallies were long and the crowd was very pro the Aussie. Three sets later Marat Safin made a comeback to win the title with Lleyton Hewitt runner up.

~

On another occasion, my New Zealand cousin emailed me saying that going to the Australian Open was on her bucket list but wasn't sure how to go about it. "You can stay with me and we can go together," I replied.

So Belinda booked her flight. "I'm happy for you to decide when we go, and I'm really looking forward to the warm weather," she wrote. Having visited Invercargill where she lives, I could relate to that, as it is very cold most of the time.

We went to several day matches and a couple of night matches, although we didn't go to the finals as the tickets were very expensive. We were able to see female and male players in Rod Laver Arena. We also went shopping at Chadstone as everything retail is much cheaper in Australia than it is in New Zealand. All her family had asked her to buy clothes, a cassette player, and games and toys for the kids. I suggested she might need to check the weight limit as she would have to pay excess or send it back as unaccompanied luggage.

As we sat chatting having a cappuccino and an apricot pastry, Belinda said "It's interesting how alike we are in interests and tastes, even though we grew up in different countries."

In fact, she was so like my sister in looks.

The family resemblance was unreal. I always favoured nurture over nature. But having met my dad's family for the first time as an adult it was obvious DNA doesn't lie.

"That's for sure," I responded.

As we passed the Australian Open shop, Belinda decided to have a look. She purchased a hat, as although she was enjoying the sunny days it was hotter than she'd expected, a t-shirt, and some smaller items, such as key rings, to give her family. I really enjoyed getting to know her. We still chat fondly about our time at the tennis.

~

My mum was from Sydney and, being a close family, we'd catch up in the holidays at my Aunt's farm in Porters Retreat, near Goulburn in New South Wales. There was a close rivalry between Melbournians and Sydneyites, as we called them. As adults, we'd meet at my cousin's house in Sydney.

I was really excited when my cousin, Sandy, mentioned that she'd like to come to the tennis. She really wanted to see Kyrgios, as did everybody else. He was playing in John

Cain arena and had the hopes of the nation on him. The fans had to queue up to get in. It wasn't unusual to stand in the queue for over an hour, and even then there was no guarantee you'd get in. He liked to play in what he called the *Peoples' court*.

"I'll stand in the queue," Sandy offered.

"Are you sure? Okay, I'll go get us a coffee."

About half an hour later, just as I arrived back, she was entering the building. A couple were leaving.

"Would you like our tickets? We're not coming back."

"Thanks so much," Sandy said as they handed her their pass.

We skipped the queue and went in to watch Kyrgios playing.

"You've just got to be in the right place at the right time," Sandy said with a smile.

All the Aussie supporters were barracking loudly, chanting "Aussie, Aussie, Aussie," to which the crowd replied "Oi, Oi, Oi!"

"Quiet please," the umpire said as he tried to control the crowd.

"Ladies and Gentlemen, please don't call out when the players are serving."

Kyrgios lost his way in the third set, throwing his racquet and getting a warning.

The game went to five sets and finished late, but we stayed to see him win.

These days there's no need to queue up outside John Cain arena because you scan the QR code. You receive a message on your mobile phone when a seat is available. The wonders of technology!

~

At my monthly hairdressing appointment, we were chatting about the tennis. "Gee I'd really like to go with you," Anna said with enthusiasm.

"I'd love to have your company, let's go early in the first week as all the courts are busy with first round players."

The first year we went she loved the atmosphere, and we watched a few games on the outside courts. Then COVID hit.

"Are we buying tickets for the Australian Open this year?" Anna asked.

"Not sure if it's going ahead. The other

grand slams have either cancelled or are not allowing spectators. I'll buy them if it's going ahead."

I texted Anna: "Get your outfit ready we're off to the tennis."

"Thumbs up," she texted back.

Bags were packed, food prepared, and water frozen. Late that afternoon I heard on the radio that Dan Andrews had announced, due to COVID, we were in lockdown again. No spectators. We were devastated as it was the next day that we were due to go! What the heck! I had been to the tennis many times but was still disappointed but it was the second time for my friend.

Even though I'd suggested we needed to be sun smart, wearing long sleeved t-shirt, hat and long trousers, the next year she was wearing a short skirt, mid-riff top and strappy gold sandals.

She knew what I was thinking and said, "Its fine, I'll apply sunblock every few hours. Anyway, you told me the seats weren't in the sun."

"Yes, but we'll be on the outside courts

where there's no cover, too."

She just smiled as we headed for the station. We caught the tram to the back entrance to the stadium. As we entered the main building we checked our tickets and made our way to the appropriate door, or so we thought. Checking our tickets the usher pointed to the area where we were to sit. I looked up at the board and thought, that's not the players we were going to see at Margaret Court arena.

"Wow, these are great seats," Anna, commented.

"I don't think we're in the right stadium."

"Really? Let's stay here anyway."

"Excuse me, would you like something to drink?" a young girl in school uniform asked.

"Say, no," I whispered in alarm. "We are in the corporate section of Rod Laver Arena."

"Cool," Anna said showing no concern. "We're here now."

"Would you like something to eat?" the young girl asked as she offered us a tray of delicious looking food.

"No, thank you," I replied for both of us

Towards the end of the day I needed to take a break. As I came back in, I stupidly came in the door closer to where we were sitting.

"Sorry, you can't go in here, your ticket is not for this stadium."

"You're kidding me, but I've been in there all day and my belongings are in there with my friend."

I was starting to feel embarrassed although I tried to stay cool. In hindsight I should have gone to the other door.

"We'll have to call security to accompany you in to get your things!"

I quickly texted Anna, letting her know what was happening. All she said was "Can we do that again next year?"

Going to the tennis with Anna became an annual event.

~

In 2023 technology had taken over and we had phone tickets. As we approached the entrance there was no barriers and gates to go through, only people asking us to check in by putting our phone to their phone. Guess what? After several attempts the woman said it wasn't working and asked us to stand aside while she found out what to do! The next guy had the same experience.

"You've got to be joking," I said. "I've paid for my tickets. I'm not standing here wasting time. I'm going in." The next day when I went to the tennis the same thing happened. I couldn't believe it.

Once in the stadium, having waited in the coffee queue, we realised the AO had gone cashless and both of us had left our credit cards at home! Standing at the side of the coffee queue, we must have looked distraught. Suddenly a lady came over and offered to buy us a coffee. "Thank you so much for doing that," Anna said, you're very kind. Here's the cash to cover the cost."

"Not at all, my shout. My husband got tickets through the company and it's costing us nothing for the day, including food and drinks. I just came down to get a break from my twins! It was a pleasure."

To this day we still laugh and say what a lovely person she was.

~

Following the death of my husband I thought I'd like to find for a new partner. I knew he'd want me to be happy, so I joined a few dating sites. It had been daunting and I was thinking I'd have some time out when I remembered I'd had a few dates with a guy called Andrew. He was very interesting. His main hobby was exploring caves across the top of Australia and mapping them. "I'm a caver," he said when we first met. I was intrigued and thought how clever he was.

I asked him if he'd be interested in coming to the tennis. He had said yes, so I wanted to look good. Now what to wear? Want to look good but don't want to get sunburnt so maybe the white shirt, with the collar and knee length blue check shorts. Of course, a hat is mandatory even though it's going to flatten my hair. It's always a dilemma as the Melbourne weather is so unpredictable. Suddenly, I changed my mind and decided to wear my favourite dress with the polka dots and a big bow just above the waist. Although it wasn't sun smart, looking good took priority!

He wasn't really into sport and hadn't

been to the tennis before. We met at the tram stop in Riversdale Road. Stepping onto the tram I noticed nearly everybody was on their way to the game. The tram stopped at the back of Rod Laver Arena, and we piled off with everyone else.

It was sunny and hot already, standing in the queue to get in, but eventually we made our way up the steps and into the cool on the stadium. It seemed like half of Melbourne was there. Entering the stadium we found our seats just in time for the start of the first game.

"Good seats," Andrew commented as the players walked onto the court.

Following the first couple of games, Andrew said, "Would you like me to get you a coffee?"

"Oh, that would be lovely, but you might be gone for quite a while with the queue and then they won't let you back in straight away."

"Not a problem."

So off he went. Very sweet, I thought, as he knew I loved a coffee.

The match was in full swing with long rallies. Both players were looking hot. Where is Andrew? I thought, feeling guilty. The queue must have been really long. As the games are going to deuce quite a lot he won't be allowed in until the change of ends. Although the game was exciting, I couldn't help wondering where he was, hoping that he hadn't got lost or decided to leave! I checked that he had taken his ticket to get back in. I wanted to ring him but phones are not allowed when the game is on. My mobile was turned to silent so I kept checking to see if he had texted me. Not a good start to our date, I thought! Eventually he got back in time to see the end of the match. As he handed me my coffee, he said, "Never doing that again."

"Sorry, I really appreciate the effort," I said with relief, thinking thankfully he hadn't left.

"Quiet please," the voice of the umpire boomed out as barrackers were shouting their support for the Aussie player. We needed a break from the tennis so we went out to get some lunch. Once we had purchased our nachos, we looked for somewhere to sit. The only thing on offer was a couple of deck chairs for patrons to watch the tennis on the big screen.

"Let's sit here," Andrew suggested.

"Okay," I replied, wishing I hadn't worn my tight dress.

Lunch was over and it was time to go back to see the next game. Andrew got up and was heading off when he looked around to see me still sitting in the deck chair.

"You'll have to give me a hand." I said sheepishly.

We both started laughing as we made our way through the crowd back to the stadium. Going home the tram was packed with fans discussing winners and losers and who might be playing tomorrow. As I looked around, I thought the fans looked exhausted from their day in the sun. A young girl who had obviously been working at the tennis was chatting to her friend. I wondered if they'd had as good a day as I had, as I noticed Andrew was holding my hand.

The Coronation Of Queen Elizabeth II

2nd June 1953

Extract from *An Aussie Backpacking Londoner 1952-1953*

Gordon Smith

How I came to be able to witness this magnificent event was a case of serendipity, one of many that I was fortunate to experience during my two years backpacking and working abroad. During my first backpacking tour in 1952, I was invited to stay with the Wagner family in Bad Ischl in the American Occupation Zone of Austria, where from their radio station, we learned of the unexpected and sad news of the death of King George VI in Sandringham. Princess Elizabeth was holidaying in Kenya when she heard the news of her father's death.

I found that I was touched deeply by the King's death, but I quickly realised how fortuitous it was for me that the death of King George VI occurred during this period of my time abroad. I was sure that next year in the spring of 1953, Queen Elizabeth II would be crowned, so I would definitely plan to be in London for that marvellous, once in a lifetime occasion.

Heinrich, the Wagner's son, asked me to explain to him what the British Royal Family meant to me, an Australian. I told him that as an Australian, I was a member of a large family called the 'British Empire', composed of many kinds of people from countries all over the world, who worked together for the common good. This also involved coming to each other's aid in times of war, famine and other troubles. It gives Australians a sense of belonging. I said that King George VI was like a father to me, and Queen Elizabeth II would be more like a sister, as we were both about the same age, and had grown up in this world in the same era. I still feel this way about her at the time of writing.

~

A month or so before the Coronation I picked up a free copy of a coloured folder put out jointly by London Transport, British Railways and the Metropolitan Police, titled; *Elizabeth R Coronation*, which I still have in my possession. It listed all the arrangements for the buses and railways in London on Coronation Day. It unfolded to show a large, coloured map of the route for the Coronation procession, which the Queen had chosen herself.

It showed that the Queen would leave Buckingham Palace, travel along The Mall, then into Northumberland Avenue, and along the Victoria Embankment, which had been reserved for children. She would then go by Bridge Street and Parliament Square into Westminster Abbey.

After she had been crowned, the procession with the Queen and Prince Phillip in their golden coach would leave the Abbey and travel along Whitehall, Cockspur Street, Pall Mall, St. James Street, and along Piccadilly to Hyde Park Corner, where it will turn into the East Carriage Road to Marble Arch, then turn right into Oxford Street, Regent Street, Haymarket, Cockspur Street and back along The Mall to Buckingham Palace.

Thursday 28th May 1953: After dinner there was panic for a while at number 22 Chesilton Road, Parson's Green where I boarded, because the small 12 inch TV had broken down! Now of all times, but my  landlady Mrs. Banks was up to the challenge. She took steps to have it repaired straight away. The fault most times and this time too, was that a valve had 'given up the ghost'.

Tuesday 2nd June: CORONATION DAY. I rose a little later than I had intended and gulped down my breakfast. Exciting and spectacular as I knew the day was going to be, it began for me in a totally unexpected and marvellous way. As I walked toward Fulham Road to catch a number 14 bus to take me to my reserved seat in a grandstand in the East Carriage Road, I saw a paperboy holding up a copy of the *Daily Express* with a banner headline that read: 'ALL THIS AND EVEREST TOO.' I bought a paper and was thrilled to read the report that Mt. Everest had just been climbed by the New Zealander

Edmund Hillary and his Sherpa, Tenzing Norgay. This news was a wonderful bonus and present for the Queen on her Coronation Day.

The credit for getting the news of the climb to London in time for the Coronation went to James Morris, a member of the expedition, who was high up on the mountain in the Western Cwm. He set out immediately to walk to Kathmandu, from where he was able to get a message through to London with the great news. The timing was perfect, but coincidental. As a young lad, I had read many books about mountaineering, many of them about attempts to climb Mt. Everest. Especially those by Frank S. Smythe, who in 1933 from Tibet, climbed higher on Everest than anyone up to that time. I was probably just as excited by this news, as by the fact that this was Coronation Day and I would soon be seeing the Coronation procession.

I found my seat in the grandstand in the East Carriage Road by 7.30 am and not long after, I was joined by my Aussie friend Ralph and his friend John. It was going to be a long wait before the procession began. There were a couple of heavy showers early in the morning, but our spirits were not dampened, and we were well rugged up. Directly behind our seat there was a large temporary stand, put up by the BBC for radio and television commentary.

It would have been great to have had a modern, small, portable radio so we could have heard what they were saying, but they were yet to be invented. There were stalls behind the stands where we could purchase drinks and food, so while we waited, we ate and drank, too many for me as it turned out. We talked to the people around us about ourselves, themselves, and where we came from. Most were Canadian and Australians. We waited patiently in exciting anticipation of what was to enfold before us.

Later in the morning the weather cleared up a little and at 11 am, a buzz went through the stands. We were told that the Queen had just left Buckingham Palace and was on her way to Westminster Abbey. The BBC commentators in the TV stand were keeping the people close by informed of what was happening, and this was being relayed to the people in our stand and other grandstands nearby. While we were waiting for the news that she had left Westminster Abbey, there were light intermittent rain showers.

Eventually, about 2.30 pm, we heard that the Queen had left Westminster Abbey, and the procession was on its way. I made sure my camera was ready, and I had a new roll of film unpacked and handy to put in the camera, when I had taken the first eight shots. It was a good half-hour, before we heard cheers coming from the direction of Hyde Park Corner. The excitement around us escalated as the cheers gradually grew louder, until at last we spotted the golden coach in the distance, unfortunately not shining in the sun, because there wasn't any. However, nothing could dull the opulence of the golden coach, flanked by the Yeomen of the Guard in their brilliant red and gold coats, breeches, and black peaked caps. The horses too were brilliantly decorated.

At last the procession was upon us and what a show it was. That coach, wow! In a matter of moments, the golden coach had passed us by, but I saw the Queen clearly with the crown on her head, because luckily she was on our side of the coach. I took a couple photos as the procession approached and when the golden coach with the Queen passed in front of us.

The long, colourful procession that followed was made up of the armies, air forces and navies of the Commonwealth countries and their bands. Of course we cheered our Australian marchers the loudest of all. At one point there was a short holdup in the procession. As luck would have it the Royal Canadian Mounted Police were halted directly in front of us for about two minutes. Their uniforms were a brilliant red, a much brighter red than I had seen in photographs and the movies. The pause gave me a chance to change over the film in the camera.

The procession took just under an hour to pass us by. It was a magnificent spectacle seeing the Queen in her gold coach and then the members of the armed forces of all the Commonwealth nations marching past with their bands.

John left and the author waiting patiently
in the grandstand

The BBC broadcasting booth just
behind where we were sitting

The Queen's Coach approaching

A close up of the Queen's coach as it passed
directly in front of our seat

The procession passing by after the
Queen's carriage

The front page of the *Daily Express* with
the procession in the background

Just after the Queen passed by, I asked Ralph
to take a photograph of the procession, with

me holding up the front page of the Daily Express showing the headline about Everest and the Coronation.

After the procession came to an end, nearly everyone from the stands spilled out onto the East Carriageway Road. Ralph, John and I walked along to Marble Arch and Oxford Street where we caught the tube to Hampstead in order to get the best view of the flyover of about 20 aircraft, which was fantastic as they emitted red, white and blue smoke. Having enjoyed seeing the flyover that didn't last very long, we then went to a café to get something to eat, but I didn't feel hungry.

After we said goodbye to John, Ralph picked up his car and we drove to see our Ausssie nurses at their flat, but I felt crook, so Ralph took me straight home. After I got into my room, I had to rush out to the toilet. I was violently ill, and collapsed into bed. That was my rather sad conclusion to a unique and exciting day. The only part of the Coronation celebrations that I regretted missing was the fireworks display at night. The day had been just too long and exciting for me, but I wouldn't have missed it for worlds. I didn't write up my diary and notebook of the fantastic Coronation Day until the following morning.

The television coverage of the Coronation was a unique event in many ways, especially the televising of the ceremony in Westminster Abbey. When the question of televising the ceremony was raised by the BBC, there was much opposition, especially by the clergy and the nobility. This was because an ancient rite decreed that only they should be present at the ceremony. However, the Queen thought otherwise. After much thought and advice, she decreed that the ceremony should be televised, because she wanted as many of her subjects as possible to witness the event.

This was the first time that TV cameras were allowed inside Westminster Abbey. There was only one stipulation—there were to be no close ups. It was estimated that the ceremony in the Abbey was viewed by 53% of the population of the UK. As there were only 2.7 million TV licences issued, each TV set must have been watched by multiple viewers.

It was thought that about 20 million people were able to watch the ceremony on the small black and white screens. An example of the multiple viewing was that Mrs. Banks had at least 10 people in the room with her to watch the event; Gwyn and Sylvia, Barbara and Chris, Brian, Auntie Maude, Mr. and Mrs. Cornish, to name a few. The wireless coverage went around the world. My family would have been listening to it back in Australia because there was no TV in Australia until just prior to the Olympic Games in Melbourne, in 1956.

At work the day after the Coronation I felt sick all day, although I finished the day okay. At night I watched replays of the Coronation ceremony in Westminster Abbey on the TV, which was most impressive.

In early July on the TV, I was thrilled to see some films of the Everest expedition. A large plaster model was used to show all the various routes up Mt Everest, including the final successful route up the Khumbu Ice Fall and the Western Cwm to the South Col which Hillary and Tenzing took to reach the 8,848 metre (29,028 ft) summit of Everest on the

29th June.

I saw John Hunt, the leader of the expedition, very English, Tenzing Norgay, the charming Sherpa porter with a beautiful smile, and of course Edmund Hillary. It was great to hear his New Zealand accent and see his boyish smile and easy manner. Also on the TV were Bourdillon and other members of the expedition. The expedition members were introduced and described a film and photographs of the successful climb. It was really exciting television.

I will never forget the events described above as long as I live.

I'll Never Forget... My Grandad is Sleeping...
Premila Thurairatnam

The night train chugged along from Colombo to Jaffna. I was asleep on the top berth of the cabin. I woke at 6 am when the train stopped at Paranthan. Beyond the carriage window, the salt mounds glistened in the dawn sunlight. I was happy that I was going to my grandad's sprawling villa nestled amidst tropical gardens in Chavakachcheri, where I'd meet my three cousins. We had such fun during the school holidays, but now my grandad was dead; he died of a stroke aged just sixty-six. I cherished my daily morning walks around the town with him, visiting the two Hindu temples. During one walk a teenager accidentally knocked me with his bike as I was holding a large teddy in my arms and couldn't see where I was walking. Grandad was furious; he slapped the boy.

Of the four cousins, I was the eldest, aged eight. An only child, I was eager for my holidays so I could play with my cousins. I was

165

shy, but precocious (even if I say so myself!), and didn't feel threatened when I was with my younger cousins. Daniel, five and Sherine, four, were siblings. Daniel was intelligent, passive and kind-hearted. Sherine loved to dress up and relax; not one for hard work. Two-year-old Varun was another only child and mischievous. He was cute and fair with brown eyes. From the minute we woke until we went to bed, it was playtime. Hide and seek, statues, jumping off the steps, cards, and the game we enjoyed most—cooking outdoors. The elder three played this game; it wasn't safe for two-year-old Varun to play with fire. We two girls would chop and cook the vegetables, delegating the hard task of keeping the fire ablaze to Daniel. He never complained and would huff and puff and blow with a pawpaw tree stem. Food cooked in the open air was scrumptious. We loved the Hindu festival of *Pongal* where Grandad would boil a pot of rice and milk outdoors, facing the rising sun; this was traditionally performed after the annual rice harvest in January as thanksgiving to the Sun.

We loved playing with the animals; a cow we helped milk, a goat, chickens from which we gathered eggs, a Dachshund named Jimmy (Grandad's pet) and a nameless cat. One morning Sherine and Varun were standing on the edge of the back verandah. Varun suddenly leapt at Sherine who tripped and fell to the ground. She cried and when an adult appeared, Varun pointed to the chicken, strutting about the verandah: "This hen pushed her!" One night, all of us cousins were seated around the dining table after dinner with a kerosene lamp[1] in the centre as there was a power cut. For some reason, we were rather quiet. Suddenly, an Eastern Barn Owl flew in through the open front door, sat in the middle of the dining table, looked around at us for about 30 seconds and flew out! We were all gobsmacked and looked at each other.

In the tropical heat, snakes visited the house in search of water. The bathroom and toilet were detached from the house. There was many a time when adults and children alike would saunter into the bathroom only to flee in terror at the sight of a long, brown snake draped over the side of the bathtub, sipping water. Snakes were frequent visitors to the chicken coop in search of chickens and eggs. Once Daniel cried, "Snake, snake!" from the front verandah, and everyone ran out to see a large, yellow rat snake slithering at breakneck speed across the front yard. The best encounter of all was a baby cobra with its head caught in a crack in the steps to the well, its body wriggling in plain sight. Kerosene oil was poured into the crack. This was how people safely removed snakes without killing them; Hindus worshipped the Cobra snake and Buddhists and Hindus didn't kill any animal; belief in reincarnation meant animals could be humans so killing animals equates to killing humans. The oil smell was a deterrent. But the snake didn't retreat. My dad, the only male in the house at the time, was called to solve the problem. He was a finicky character who washed his hands thoroughly many times a day and took long baths—this job was not for him, but he came anyway. He held the snake's body with a piece of paper and pulled it out with much ado, whilst the rest of the family watched in suspense. The snake had a toad in its mouth, it had gone into the crack to devour it.

Terrified though people were of snakes, a hundred years prior, Sir Emerson Tennent, colonial secretary of Ceylon, who conducted a diligent study of the island, references *Life and Adventures in Ceylon* by Wolf, where rat snakes were so domesticated by the natives as to feed at their table. Quote: "I once saw an example of this in the house of a native. It being mealtime, he called his snake, which immediately came forth from the roof under which he and I were sitting. He gave it *victuals* from his own dish, which the snake took of itself from off a fig leaf that was laid for it, and ate along with its host. When it had eaten its fill, he gave it a kiss and bade it go to its hole."[2]

Most evenings we cousins, accompanied by an adult, would cross the railway track to play in the dunes and munch delectable fish cutlets. We passed a temple for a malevolent god where screaming was believed to drive out evil spirits. People brought their disease-ridden family members (usually mentally ill) to be cured. On the way, we'd visit the station master's house where we could climb out of the window onto the Mansard roof and watch the signal being pulled and the trains go by. At night we'd take our dinner of crab curry and *puttu*, go up to the rooftop terrace of Grandad's home and eat under the stars. I could reach out from the terrace and pluck mangoes from one of the five varieties of mango trees in the grounds. I'd peel and suck them with the juice dribbling down my chin.

This was our first funeral. I knew that Grandad had died. Sherine and Varun were too young to comprehend. Daniel's mother told him Grandad was simply asleep, to avoid alarming him, and he believed her. Many people came to attend the funeral at the house; Grandad had been a successful lawyer, and the townsfolk were paying their respects. Grandad's body lay in an open casket in the main hall of the house. He was dressed in a black suit with a posy in his pocket, bald and serene. We watched him and our sad parents with apprehension. The next morning a group of women gathered in a circle, embracing each other, their bodies bent forwards, and wailing.

We didn't know this at the time, but these women were the Professional Mourners—women of lower caste, hired by the funeral house to lament the *oppari* according to custom[3,4,5]. When a relative of the deceased entered the house, the women would be tipped off and wail even louder! The more mourners, the higher the status in society of the deceased. During the funeral service, we held candles and stood around the coffin with a sense of foreboding. Varun sniffled and insisted that his dad carry him; when his dad needed to be a pallbearer, Varun clung to him, wailing. Daniel watched a lanky beggar named *Chinnakutty* (meaning small baby!) who stood weeping by the coffin; Grandad had been good to him, and Daniel expected Grandad to wake up and give him some money. The house and grounds were overflowing with people, seated on chairs and on the ground. A lawyer gave an enthralling tribute; he gave an account of Grandad's achievements and praised his commitment to serving the community. 'The town market is a lasting monument to his initiative, zeal and spirit of service and he will go down in history as this town's first urban council chairman'; the crowd cheered.

When the funeral service ended, the coffin was carried in procession to the cemetery. Our great-grandmother was buried there, too. Each holiday the family looked forward to the ritual of visiting her grave in the local graveyard located out of town. We'd walk through the rice paddy fields, along the bunds, witnessing a glorious sunset, enjoying the gentle evening breeze, and spotting birds. Once our grandmother had walked on ahead; when we approached the grave, we saw the tail end of her sky-blue saree flap behind the tombstone of our great-grandmother. Everyone panicked, thinking it was a ghost, only to find it was Grandma! After we paid our respects, we'd return home by the road; it was too dark to walk in the paddy fields. We'd listen to the eerie calls of seagulls. We'd stop and buy hot *kothu roti*—chopped roti fried with beef pieces, eggs and vegetables—and return home contented.

The burial was attended by males only. This practice originated with the aristocrats in eighteenth-century England, where upper-class women were not allowed to be part of the funeral procession or burial as they may not restrain their grief which would be embarrassing to the stoic calmness they were meant to portray; men could be trusted not to display strong emotion. This culture was soon taken up by the rest of the upper classes in England and its colonies[6].

When the priest concluded the last rites, an adult took the two little boys and walked away. Daniel turned back and saw the coffin being lowered into the prepared grave. *Oh No! they're burying Grandad, I'm never going to see him again!* The shock continues to haunt him half a century later. However young a child, some events are imprinted in memory, captured like photographs. A lesson for adults—best to tell children the truth.

A week after the funeral, a lunch called *Selavu* was given by the family to the townsfolk. This was a cultural custom—giving thanks to the people who had brought food to the funeral house during the funeral week; a grieving family had no time to cook. Sherine, although just four at the time, recalls how she saw people *everywhere* and ladies in the backyard cooking in *humungous* pots. Curious that she remembers this lunch and not the funeral. A few days later, Jimmy the Dachshund moped around howling, with tears in his eyes; he died at the end of the week and was buried in the house grounds.

This story is based on the author's childhood experiences.

Footnotes:

1. This is the lamp that was on the table, now in my home in Melbourne.
2. Wikipedia: Professional mourning originates from Egyptian, Chinese, Mediterranean and Near Eastern

cultures going back to biblical times.

3. Alagu Subramaniam, 'Professional Mourners' short story in *The Big Girl* book, 1964, reprint 2018.
4. EA Gamini Fonseka, Servile Mourning for the Powerful: A Critical Reading of 'Professional Mourners' by Alagu Subramaniam (2014), www.academia.edu
5. Tennent J. E, *Ceylon Volume 1*, 1859.
6. A good blog post researching this topic by Kathryn Kane: https://regencyredingote.wordpress.com/2013/10/18/the-regency-way-of-death-ladies-at-funerals/

Glossary:

Oppari – an ancient form of lamenting in South India and North East Sri Lanka. It's a folk song tradition and is an admixture of eulogy and lament

Puttu – means 'portioned' in Tamil and is made of steamed cylinders of ground rice layered with coconut shavings

Victuals – old English for food provisions

About the Authors

Robert Eisler

Robert is a poet who loves the power of the written word. He regularly shares his poetry on his Instagram account: roberteislerpoetry

Katharina Fares

Katharina Fares was born in Hungary into the tenth generation of German-speaking settlers. She grew up in Communist East of Germany and moved to West Germany where she studied fashion design and clothing manufacturing.

After coming to Australia she worked in the fashion industry, and then began her own manufacturing business and established a number of retail shops.

Later on she obtained a Dip. Ed. and a B. Ed. and lectured in her field of expertise. During this time she wrote accredited curriculum documents for three occupational streams in clothing manufacturing.

Her novel, *View from a Barred Window* is based on her own experiences but it is also the story of thousands of displaced people.

Sakuntala Gananathan

Sakuntala is a retired chartered accountant. Her historical novel *White Flowers of Yesterday* was published in the US and was awarded Editor's Choice by her publishers, iUniverse Inc.

An excerpt of their appraisal: "The author has done a fantastic job of weaving setting, characterisation, historical information, dialogue and plot together to create a complete, unique and compelling story…" while Kirkus Review wrote "…a surfeit of grace and wit…"

Sakuntala takes an active interest in the

Tamil Senior Citizens Fellowship (Victoria) Inc, a non-profit association. She is also a member of the Australian Tamil Literary and Arts Society Inc., Casey Tamil Manram, and Tamil Senior Citizen Benevolent Society, all based in Victoria. In 2013, her short story, *Mend a Bend*, earned her a prize at the Monash WordFest Short Story Competition.

Lenette Griffin

Lenette is a retired accountant who has lived in leafy south-eastern Melbourne for over fifty years, close to her two sons and three granddaughters.

She likes nothing better than hiding away with a good book, classical music, with a preference for opera, writing and overseas travel, particularly throughout Europe, although she has travelled widely throughout Australia.

Her love of rural and outback Australia is the result of growing up in the big-tree country of Western Australia, a sixth-generation eldest daughter of a large farming family. She has an on-going passion for residential property investing in different states but is now firmly focussed on travelling for research – for her coming novels, of course.

Marlene Laurent

Born in Australia, Marlene grew up in the post-war suburb of South Oakleigh. Brought up a Catholic, she entered the convent at the age of seventeen after attending boarding school in Fremantle, WA. She left the convent following the Ecumenical Council when changes were implemented in the Catholic Church.

Teaching became a passion. She was actively involved in education in the Victorian system and implemented many changes to the curriculum during her career. She became an Assistant Principal at Brandon Park Primary and then Principal at Oakwood Park Primary and finally at Glenferrie Primary. She played basketball and tennis and attended the gym regularly to keep fit.

On retiring she decided to have a go at writing; a lifelong dream. She is a member of the Caulfield Writer's Group and the Monash Writer's Group. This short story is her fifth for the Monash Writer's Group anthologies.

Marlene lives in East Bentleigh and spends her time cycling, keeping fit at the local gym, reading, writing and travelling. She is a member of the Australian Conservation Association, The Wilderness Society and other conservation groups. Her memoir, *Down the Road to Waterford* is out now.

Sung-Ju Suya Lee

Suya received a BFA from York University, Canada, an MBA from Bradford University School of Management, UK, and a PhD in Media & Communication from RMIT University, Australia. As part of her creative practice PhD, she wrote a farce comedy screenplay, *The Wedding Jackpot*, which was long-listed for the ScreenCraft Comedy screenplay contest.

The poems were inspired by Ernest Hemingway's famous quote, "There is nothing to writing. All you do is sit down at a typewriter and bleed."

Besides being a "forever" student and travelling, she has had many "day" jobs over the decades to support her writing, filmmaking, and acting career. She feels privileged to be a part of the Monash Writers Group.

Robert New

When he was in high school, a dare escalated a little too quickly and Robert made the state final in an interpretive dance competition. Thankfully, his teacher was okay with him chickening out of the main event, thus preserving his affection for education. Whilst not a direct consequence, Robert has since spent too much of his life studying and has just embarked upon his seventh university degree, a PhD in Education. Robert has degrees in psychology, sociology, biology and education, all of which inspire his writing, which has been described as "educational of the human condition", and "smart and imaginative".

Robert is kosmemophobic, meaning he has a fear of jewellery. He has no idea why, it just freaks him out.

Robert's books include *Incite Insight*, *MoveMind* and *Colours of Death: Sergeant Thomas'*

Casebook. His latest novel, *Sovereign Assassin* was meant to be satire about how the world would respond to a leader who killed people but now seems increasingly plausible.

Andy Russell

For much of his working life Andy Russell was involved with research into intelligent robotics. Some of his robots communicate using puffs of air, lick the floor to follow chemical trails or burrow through the ground searching for chemical leaks. Reviewers sometimes complained his research was too speculative, perhaps too much like science fiction? Now, retired, he has the freedom to explore robotics and science fiction more broadly without any requirement to demonstrate practical implementations. The future of technology promises many exciting developments as well as complex ethical considerations. Science fiction provides an ideal medium for investigating the possibilities. His debut novel *Intelligent Consent* was released in 2020 and was followed by a sequel, *Intelligence Horizon* in 2022.

Dilys Smith

Dilys has had a lifelong interest in writing poetry and was please when this anthology gave her the opportunity to publish some of her poems.

Gordon J R Smith

Gordon was born in 1927 in Victoria. He qualified as a tradesman fitter and turner in 1949, with the Victorian Railways. He was a Rover Scout, and member of the Youth Hostels Association. In 1952, he sailed abroad to the UK on a working and backpacking holiday, returning to Australia in 1953. He worked, married and raised a family on the Kiewa Hydro-Electric Scheme for ten years. Returning to Melbourne, he worked for eighteen years with General Electric. When GE closed, he taught Fluid Power at the Royal Melbourne Institute of Technology, from where he retired in 1993. He has written and published books about his travels abroad and working life.

Premila Thurairatnam

Premila was born in the north of idyllic Sri Lanka and grew up in the capital, Colombo. Aged 19, she married a radio officer and sailed on two ships over 2 years. Her short story based on this experience was published in the 2022 anthology. She emigrated to Australia in 1991. She completed her BSc (Hons) at Monash University and worked at two global pharmaceutical companies for 15 years then consulted for pharmaceutical, medical device & cannabis companies for 4 years. She is now a teaching associate at Monash University for Chemistry undergraduates.

An avid reader, she loves to craft words and aspires to become a writer. She has edited and republished two of her granduncle's short story books which form part of the South Asian Collection in the British Library, the State Library of Victoria, the National Library, Canberra, and the Monash Public Library. She has researched his life in England in the 1930s and published two biographical articles. She has written about Ceylon Furniture and Ivory Artefacts for the *Ceylon Society of Australia* magazine. Her contribution to this anthology was short-listed in the Monash Wordfest short story competition in 2021.

Erica Tippett

Erica's love of story was developed as a child. She has fond memories of her dad reading bedtime stories to her. When her dad passed she decided life was too short to think or talk about the things you want to do. It was time for action. Erica's debut novel, *Unsuited*, resulted from that critical shift in mind set. She also began working with her two kids on a middle-grade (suitable for children 7-12 years old) chapter book series. She is in the process of publishing *The Teleporting Twins* 8-book series under J.A. Tippett. Learn more at ericatippett.com.

The Way Forward

The follow up to the Monash Writers Group anthology, Unprecedented Times. This time the authors have taken the theme of 'the way forward' and used it to craft a diverse and compelling collection of stories and poems.

ISBN: 9780994439963
Available to order from bookshops and online retailers including Amazon.com.
https://amzn.to/3XWZ1V1

The theme of this anthology is Unprecedented Times. Not all the stories relate to the events of 2020, some are historical and others futuristic.

The contributors write in a variety of genres, so there is sure to be something in this collection for every reader.

ISBN 9780648038627
Available to order from bookshops and online retailers including Amazon.com.
https://amzn.to/3rs9rMI

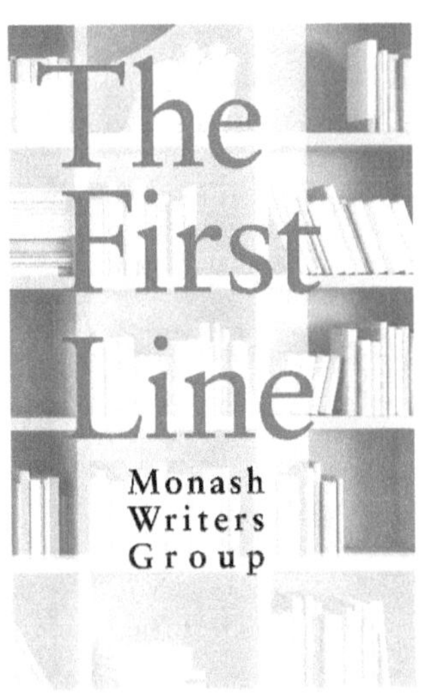

This is a short story anthology by the Monash Writers Group. Each writer has taken the **first** line of a story they like and used it as the starting point for a new tale.

Some lines are famous, others obscure, but the works they have inspired are original and entertaining.

From historical fiction, drama, science fiction, mystery, adventure and literary there is a story in this collection for every reader.

ISBN 9780648327332

Available to order from bookshops and online retailers including Amazon.com.

https://amzn.to/2oNiLDj

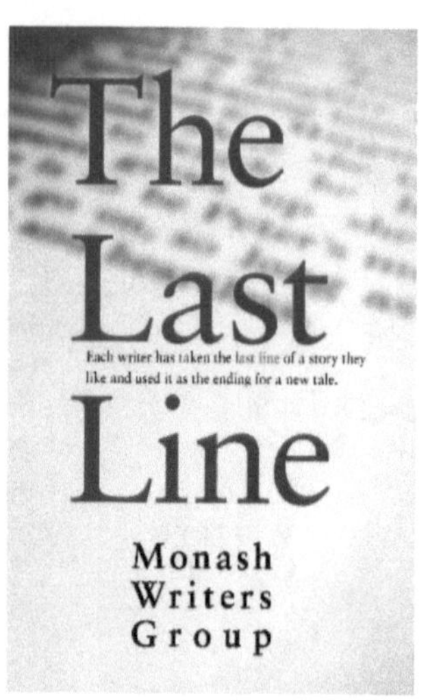

Each writer has taken the **last** line of a story they like and used it as the ending line for a new tale. Some lines are famous, others obscure, but the works they've inspired are original and entertaining.
From historical fiction, drama, science fiction, mystery and literary there is a story in this collection for every reader.

ISBN 9780648327394
Available to order from bookshops and online retailers including Amazon.com.
https://amzn.to/427eDHX